A MURDER ON THE CÔTE D'AZUR

PENELOPE BANKS MURDER MYSTERIES
BOOK 12

COLETTE CLARK

DESCRIPTION

A riveting Riviera murder!

Antibes 1926
Penelope "Pen" Banks and friends have finally made it to
the Côte d'Azur, settling into a beautiful villa in Antibes.
After only one week it's been perfect weather, beautiful
scenery, welcoming French locals, and a fashionable set of
American expats with whom to socialize.

The only fly in the ointment is the odious Mrs. Vera Tynehook. With her belittling words, acerbic nature, and ruthless
lack of consideration for others, she has managed to make an
enemy of almost everyone.
It's enough for Penelope to wonder why so many attend the
parties she hosts, no matter how swanky they are. She soon
learns they all have a bit of fun at the hostess's expense. But
what happens when a night of harmless teasing ends in
Vera's murder?

There are too many suspects to count, especially when the police reveal the surprising nature of her death.

Murder on the Côte d'Azur is the twelfth book in the Penelope Banks Murder Mysteries series set in the 1920s. Join her and her friends as they begin their European adventure.

CHAPTER ONE

ANTIBES 1926

"I see I'm not the only one up at this ungodly hour of the day. I suppose your plans are as villainous as mine?"

Penelope "Pen" Banks turned at the sound of a somewhat familiar voice. She and her friends had been on the Côte d'Azur for only one week, settling into a lovely villa in Antibes. Even new faces were as familiar to her as old friends, thanks to her condition which remembered everything like a colorized photograph.

Thus, Penelope easily recognized Estelle Summers skipping along the cobblestone street of Old Antibes to catch up with her. Her brunette Eton crop was almost hidden underneath her large sun hat. She wore a loose, open jacket and pajama bottoms over her bathing suit. From one shoulder hung a large straw tote.

"Villainous?" Pen echoed.

Estelle grinned. "Why else would you sneak out of the house without any of your interesting friends in tow?"

Yes, Penelope had left without the others—Cousin Cordelia, Benny Davenport, Lucille "Lulu" Simmons, and Richard Prescott, a detective with the NYPD—but only because they were still asleep. The prior night had been gin martinis and several lively rounds of charades that went on well past midnight.

Estelle pouted. "You didn't even bother bringing along that handsome beau of yours, the good detective. I find men with scars so dashing." She eyed Penelope's hand. "Or is he something more?"

Pen reflexively held up her hand, fingers splayed, to admire the ring Richard had given her when he proposed. It had a gray pearl abutted by two small jade insets. It was perfect. Their voyage across the Atlantic to get to France had been rather tumultuous, even beyond how fatal it had been.

This first week in Antibes had done a wonderful job of calming the waters. She and Richard were closer than ever, as they'd enthusiastically confirmed with one another whenever they had a moment to themselves.

When in France....

"Ah yes, most definitely something more," Estelle said with a laugh as she caught Pen's smile. An apologetic look came to her face. "I hope I'm not ruining your bit of morning solitude. I do enjoy Sawyer, but even I need some time alone. Besides, there's something perfectly divine about having the beach all to myself before it's infested with us awful Americans."

"We do seem to have taken over, haven't we?" Pen agreed.

"Indeed. Though, it's also nice to get ahead of the most brutal parts of the day. You'd think a girl from California would be used to the sun, but no, it still wears on me so. Too much Scottish blood running through my veins." Estelle lifted one arm to inspect it as the loose sleeve pooled toward her elbow. The pale skin and fine layer of nearly invisible hair with a slight ruddy tinge lent credence to her Scottish origins.

She just as quickly dropped her arm, the sleeve falling back into place. "I can hurry on to the shore if you'd rather be alone."

Truthfully, Penelope would have preferred being alone. She enjoyed this wee hour of the day, walking along the narrow cobblestone streets of Old Antibes. She admired the way the French seemed to leisurely take their time unlocking doors and opening shutters to begin their day. It was a far cry from the hustle and bustle of Manhattan, where people walked in a quick step and cars blared their horns at all hours if drivers were delayed by so much as a half-second.

She decided a few minutes of company wasn't too terrible. Of the few people she'd met so far, she found Estelle quite agreeable. She was vivacious and not concerned with the usual decorum when it came to meeting new people. Perhaps Californians were just more casual with their introductions. Pen hadn't quite caught where her "companion," Sawyer Hendricks was from, but Estelle was from a city called Santa Barbara. Her family had made their money in oil that had been discovered there.

"Applesauce, I don't mind the company."

"Well then," Estelle said, easily slipping her free arm through Penelope's. "I get to be the one to tell everyone I learned a little something about our most recent arrivals. Shame on you for not hosting a party by now."

"We've only been here a week, and—"

Estelle's laughter interrupted her. "I'm only teasing, darling. I don't blame you for keeping to yourselves to begin with. I'm just a Nosy Nellie who likes to learn all about people. My appetite is voracious, I should warn you. So tell me something interesting about yourself I can diffuse among the expats to seem more interesting by proxy."

"There's really nothing interesting to tell."

"Hogwash, everyone has been atwitter about that horrid murder that took place on your voyage here. Someone *that* famous being killed? The scuttlebutt is you were actively involved in solving it."

"Well..." Penelope certainly didn't want her only reputation in Antibes to be related to murder. Yes, she'd become a private investigator back in New York, but she had hoped to hang that hat up while she was on holiday in Europe. "I just happened to be nearby when it happened."

"Ahh, I can tell when someone would rather change the subject. How about I give you all the gossip about Antibes instead? That seems fair."

"If you insist," Penelope certainly wasn't going to argue against learning more about the city where she'd be spending the next few months.

"I *can* tell you Vera Tynehook is *quite* perturbed at your snub."

Penelope pressed her lips together in silence rather than express her opinion on that particular woman. She had received an invitation to Mrs. Tynehook's party welcoming her to Antibes. It was to be held at the Hôtel de Platine, situated on a jutting cluster of cliffs with a commanding view of the Riviera. Sadly, the invitation had deliberately excluded one member of Pen's household. Penelope hadn't told her friend Lucille "Lulu" Simmons that she hadn't been invited, most likely due to her race. Instead, Pen had just sent a very curt, "No, thank you," in return.

Estelle smiled knowingly. "My thoughts exactly. Vera is an insufferably odious woman. Many of us applauded you in secret. She doesn't understand the way things are done in

France. Or perhaps she does, and just doesn't care...until you, that is." Estelle laughed with gay delight. "I'd wager there was enough steam in the Tynehook household to fuel the Orient Express after you declined. Perhaps you'll be the one to give her a good lesson on French manners."

Penelope was surprised to hear someone be so frank about their thoughts on Vera Tynehook. Most of the people she'd met thus far had been circumspect about it, but she'd sensed plenty of animosity toward the woman. One would assume most of them would also decline party invitations from her. And yet she seemed to be the hostess *du jour* for Antibes.

"Why *does* anyone attend her parties if she's so hated?"

"Aside from her presence, Vera's parties really are the most fabulous *soirées*. She has money coming out of her ears, you know. That allows her to buy a lot of favor, especially among the more interesting Americans, i.e. those with no money, but plenty of talent. They are the ones who have to sing for their dinner. She'll even allow them rooms at the Hôtel de Platine despite the ongoing renovations, though only in the servants' quarters, mind you."

"Allow?"

"She owns it, didn't you know? Bought it in late spring. Has aims to make it the most luxurious hotel along the Riviera. Only the finest for Madame Tynehook."

"That's a shame. I rather like how quaint it is now," Pen lamented. A perfectly clear image of the hotel as it was only a week ago, in a lovely shade of coral, appeared in her head. There was a rustic charm to it, like a crumbling estate that didn't put on airs and thus appealed to everyone, no matter their class.

"Vera has a desperate need to be at the center of things, you see. Particularly if she can situate herself on a pedestal at the same time. It's the sole reason she bought the hotel, you see. So many Americans called it home. It's also why she hosts so many parties. I will say, her poor beleaguered assistant, Julia, is an absolute maestra at pulling together a fine mix of interesting people, delicious food, endless champagne, and fabulous entertainment. I honestly don't know how she does it. Of course, we all make a sport out of adding even more entertainment." One green eye winked conspiratorially, but offered no explanation. "Oh, and then there's Peter Compton. He always makes a grand appearance. We suspect there is some bit of scandalous dirt Vera has used to blackmail him into performing. He finds her as repugnant as the rest of us. In fact, he usually...well, you have to be there to appreciate it."

"Peter Compton?" Penelope's curiosity was officially piqued. She was familiar with the songwriter, who had produced a number of popular musicals. His songs always had a humorous bent to them, filled with double entendres and sarcastic wit. "What exactly happens at these parties?"

"Oh no, no, no," Estelle laughed, wagging her finger. "I'm going to tease you with it in hopes you'll save us all by coming to her next party." She noted Penelope's expression of reluctance. "Oh, don't worry, Vera won't make the same mistake again. By refusing an invitation, you've become the most interesting American here. She'll fall over herself to re-invite you and *all* of your company. I suggest you accept this time. Trust me, it will be worth it."

Before Penelope could try prying anything more out of her, Estelle's attention was caught by something just past her shoulder.

"I see we have a little rebel on our hands." Estelle smirked with a knowing look.

Penelope turned her head to follow her gaze. She saw a

very pretty, young blonde woman, probably just barely eighteen. She was smiling in a coquettish manner with a young man whose back was to them. The large apron over his workman's clothing exposed him as a local, probably a stockroom boy in one of the shops. The girl hadn't yet noticed her two observers, her flirtatious gaze reserved for only one person in the world. She tilted her head and began playing with her hair. The lovely bouquet of lavender in her hands, tied with a ribbon, was no doubt the reason for her admiration.

"That's Lily, Vera's daughter. The favorite, even though she's adopted. Poor Prynne, she's the older sister —*not* adopted. The way that awful woman treats them both...."

Penelope heard the disdain in Estelle's voice. It made her all the more glad she hadn't accepted the invitation. Still, she and her friends were in Antibes for the summer; they couldn't avoid Vera forever. Estelle had succeeded in planting a seed of curiosity about the Tynehooks, particularly these parties of Vera's.

Lily reached out to rest a hand on the young man's arm, a gesture that girls learned early on was the quickest way to a boy's heart. That's when she noticed Estelle and Penelope watching them. Instantly a frown came to her face and alarm touched her eyes. She spoke in a fervent manner, which had the young man turning to glance their way. Penelope could see why Lily was so smitten. He was attractive in that way rebellious young women preferred—handsome features, defiance and insolence written all over his face, all melded into the perfect specimen to give any mother heart palpitations. Lily grabbed his arm and dragged him around a corner and out of sight.

"Now you know why I like rising early." Estelle laughed

with amusement. "My own private wilderness walk to observe the local flora and fauna during mating season. Mother Nature never fails to entertain."

"I take it Mrs. Tynehook is not so pleased with Mother Nature's designs?"

"Vera has that poor girl's entire life plotted and planned to excruciating detail. She'll soon be married. There's an earl or something waiting in the wings. Vera's an unapologetic anglophile and, as you already know, elitist to a prejudicial degree."

Penelope felt her umbrage at the woman deepen. How sad to have one's life controlled in such a manner. Penelope's father had been strict, but not to that degree. At least he had allowed her to choose her own future husband, disaster that it had almost been.

"Well, I suppose I should leave you to your day. I'm sure we'll run into one another soon enough. Ta-ta!" Estelle released Penelope's arm and trotted off toward the shore. She turned to give one final parting grin. "Accept the next invitation, it'll be the cat's pajamas. Trust me!"

Pen watched her go, and a cynical smile came to her face. She had to admit, that seed of curiosity was already sprouting in her head. Perhaps she *would* accept Vera's next invitation.

CHAPTER TWO

Penelope admired the large white villa from a distance as she returned from her morning excursion. It had a perfect view down to the water, especially from the balcony of the room she shared with Richard. Vines with bright pink bursts of bougainvillea clung to the exterior and lent a floral scent to the air.

She had done a bit of shopping during her early morning excursion and returned home, arms filled with her purchases. Finding freshly made baguettes so early hadn't been a problem. However, she'd happily stumbled upon a flower shop open early and purchased a bouquet of lavender, inspired by the similar bunch Lily had. She'd also coaxed a shopkeeper to sell her a pair of espadrilles and a painted scarf, even though his store wouldn't open for another two hours.

"Ah, Irma," she said, greeting the housemaid she'd hired for their stay in Antibes. "Can you find a vase for these flowers while I take these shoes and scarf up to my room? I'm sure there's one tucked away somewhere. I'm famished, so I'm going to tuck into this baguette. Please give it to

Berthe to put in the solarium with some butter and jam."
Berthe was the cook who came by each day to prepare their
meals.

"Oui, Mademoiselle Banks. I believe Madame Davies is
already at breakfast."

"Well, I suppose I should quickly get refreshed and join
her."

Penelope returned to her large bedroom to find Richard
awake and getting dressed. She admired his handsome face
as he combed his dark hair. The scar that ran down the right
side of his jaw just below the ear to his neck was a souvenir
from the plane crash he'd suffered as a pilot during the
Great War. Estelle was right, it was rather dashing.

"I see you're back from your secret tryst with Pierre. Or
is it Jean-Paul?" One dark eye with long lashes winked
at her.

"So you weren't worried when you woke and found me
gone? For all you know I could have been abducted in the
night."

"I pity the man who kidnaps you."

She scowled at him, then joined him when he laughed.
"Cousin Cordelia is already at breakfast. I bought a few
loaves of fresh baguettes for us to enjoy."

Penelope slipped out of her morning clothes and threw
on the black silk, floral kimono draped over a chair. She'd
change into her beach attire after breakfast.

Cousin Cordelia was in fact already seated in the solarium, where they'd taken to enjoying informal breakfasts.
Blessedly, Pen eyed a pot of coffee and a carafe of juice to go
with the toast and eggs her cousin was already enjoying.
The baguettes were laid out with jam and butter as
instructed. Irma had also found a vase for the flowers, and
they added a cheerful lavender touch to the morning.

"Good morning, cousin," Pen sang.

"Ah Penelope, you're finally up. I don't know how you young people stay in bed all day."

Even though Penelope had been gone for a while, it was still only mid-morning. Benny, a notorious night owl, wouldn't dare rise before noon without a good reason. Lulu was used to singing jazz during evening hours, but she wasn't quite that bad about mornings. Still, they were on holiday, and there was no reason to pressure anyone to rise before they were ready.

"I went out and did a bit of shopping. Hence the baguettes and flowers," she said, as she and Richard took seats at the table.

"All alone? In a strange, foreign city?" Cousin Cordelia looked at her in mild alarm.

Pen laughed as she tore off the end of a baguette. "Not to worry, I had company. Estelle Summers was taking advantage of the early hour as well to enjoy the shore in solitude."

"Such an interesting couple she and her beau are, though I didn't see wedding rings. I suppose that's the French way, to live together without taking vows," Cousin Cordelia said, sighing as though she had finally come to accept these newfangled customs among the young. She had come from the generation of Penelope's father, and still held onto old-fashioned beliefs.

Penelope and Richard eyed each other with subtle smiles. Cousin Cordelia had been surprisingly silent on the issue of them sharing a bedroom. Perhaps the engagement ring made it more palatable.

"We only talked briefly." Pen paused before continuing. "She thinks Vera Tynehook will be sending another invitation for a party, this time with *everyone* included."

"Surely, we won't accept?" Cousin Cordelia scoffed. She had been the one who had first seen the invitation in the small stack of mail shortly after their arrival. After opening it and noting one glaring omission, Pen had of course told Richard. Thus, everyone presently at the table knew about Vera's snub of Lucille. Pen was pleased to see that her cousin's gradual path to progressive thinking had easily allowed her to accept Lulu as part of their European tour. She was even more pleased to see how firmly she defended her against such slights.

"Estelle seemed to hint that it would be worthwhile to accept. The parties, by all accounts, are quite the bee's knees. And apparently, everyone in Antibes takes issue with the woman, even her own daughters, poor things. I suspect Mrs. Tynehook is made the donkey of the show. Normally, I'd be opposed to such nastiness, but in her case, I'll make an exception. Peter Compton can be counted on to perform, Estelle told me."

"Peter Compton?" Richard's brow rose with appreciation. "He alone makes it worthwhile."

"Is he the one that produced that musical, *Ladies and Gentlemen*? I hear it was rather...bawdy." Cousin Cordelia pursed her lips disapprovingly.

"And just when I was beginning to suspect your sensibilities were modernizing, Cousin," Pen teased with a laugh. "It's no more bawdy than any vaudeville act. He just has a way with words is all. You never know if he's singing something perfectly innocent or perfectly...bawdy, I suppose."

"I say if you have to wonder, assume the worst."

"In which case, we definitely have to accept the next invitation. I wouldn't mind a bit of bawdiness while I'm here. And who doesn't love a party?" Pen laughed at Cousin Cordelia's censuring look.

"What's this about a party?" Lulu's voice, sounding like the purr of a cat even first thing in the morning, came from the entrance to the solarium.

Penelope smiled and waved for her to sit down with them. "You're up earlier than expected."

"It's all this fresh air. Without smoke and grime and dirt, my head just isn't right," she said with a grin as she sat and reached for the coffee pot.

"Mine either," Pen agreed. "It must be all the salt from the sea because I've been having such a craving for fish. I think I'll have Berthe buy some kippers or anchovies to mix in my eggs."

Richard and Lulu weren't shy about expressing their thoughts on that, both frowning with distaste.

Cousin Cordelia was of a different mind. "Perhaps every now and again, it might be a nice addition. Fish is good for the liver. Not every day of course, too much causes a touch of the dementia, I've heard," Cousin Cordelia cautioned. It's the residue from ships and bombs in the water from that dreadful war."

Penelope, Richard, and Lulu exchanged brief looks of amusement.

"As for the party, a little bird told me this morning that we might be getting our first invite while we're here. I've been told it's one not to be missed," Penelope explained to Lulu.

"With Americans?" Lulu gave her a skeptical look.

"We're in France, Lulu. Americans come here because they crave something different. You needn't worry about certain stiff-collared prejudices. Here, we're all artists, bohemians, lovers."

"Goodness, Penelope, you make us sound like

debauched libertines." Cousin Cordelia looked perfectly scandalized.

"And why not?" Pen laughed. "You won't find anyone measuring the length of your bathing suits to make sure you don't show too much thigh on the beaches here. Speaking of, let's get to the beach soon. I want to secure a good spot. That is, if Benny manages to wake before the sun sets."

Benny was up by noon. After a glass of champagne and the last bit of baguette, he proclaimed himself fit for sunbathing. By then, Irma had packed everything needed for a day on the shore.

There was little space left for them to set up camp when they reached the water, so they etched out a spot closer to the sea. After only a week, almost every face Penelope saw surrounding them was as familiar to her as those of her oldest friends.

"Honestly, only France could get me to sit in what is essentially dirt," Benny groused. He wore white, wide-legged linen pants and a small wrap that looked like a short kimono on top. Underneath a wide-brimmed hat, small round sunglasses were perched on his nose. "I'm accompanying you all solely for the views of my fellow animals in the wild. Perhaps I'll hear the bird calls of some delightful gossip."

"I'm staying right by your side, dear boy," Lulu said, her arm in his. "I prefer to *admire* the sea, not bathe in it."

"Zounds, you two. We come all the way to the Riviera from New York, and we might as well be on Coney Island for all you take advantage of it."

"Nonsense, I for one am enjoying the legal alcohol," Lulu said with a grin.

"Hear, hear, dove," Benny agreed.

"I plan on enjoying water that isn't freezing. A good daily swim should keep me from getting too soft while I'm here," Richard said. He began setting up their little camp, laying down blankets, and opening their umbrellas.

"I may wade in a bit...perhaps up to my knees," Cousin Cordelia said primly.

"That's the spirit! I fully plan on taking a dip." Pen jumped to her feet and began stretching in anticipation of a short swim.

She glimpsed Estelle, half-hidden underneath the large umbrella protecting her upper body from the sun. Her pajama bottoms covered the lower half. Sawyer lay prone next to her in nothing more than his swimming outfit, drinking in the rays of sunshine. He had a lean, tanned body, and his hair was bleached by the sun.

They were next to the Martells, who were the original settlers of the French Riviera—at least as far as the American invasion. Both in their mid-thirties, they had been the first to make it their permanent, year-round home, settling in during a season when the French and the rest of Europe fled back to their native habitats. Since then, more and more Americans had trickled in. They'd eventually made enough of an impression that the local French community had no choice but to accommodate them.

Estelle espied Penelope from beneath her sunhat and waved her over to join their little quartet.

"I'll be right back," she said to everyone before making her way through the golden sand to meet the two couples. Curiosity had gotten the better of her.

"I think it's high time you *formally* meet everyone,

starting with the stars of the show, Finlay and George Martell," Estelle said, gesturing to the couple next to her. "This is the enigmatic Penelope Banks. I've persuaded her to attend one of Vera's parties."

The pinched look on the faces of the Martells at the mention of Vera's name told her Estelle had been right about the universal sentiment toward the woman. They eased into welcoming smiles as their eyes settled on Penelope.

Finlay might have been pretty if not for how thin and sallow she seemed. Compared to the golden tans and bodies in the pink of health surrounding them, she seemed an odd addition. Her blonde hair was thin and her pale blue eyes were watery and sunken above dark circles. Perhaps her health had brought them to the South of France, where the sea air would do her some good. Still, it was difficult to imagine her with a man like George, who was dashingly handsome in an almost rugged sort of way. His dark, brown hair was windswept in a frivolous manner. It fit with the skin that had turned perfectly brown from years of worshiping the sun.

"Very nice to meet you, Mrs. Martell," Pen said, reaching her hand out to shake.

"Heavens, don't call me Mrs. Martell," Finlay said, her face brightening into a smile that made her quite lovely. "My husband might get the idea I should be a proper wife. Finlay will do."

"And I'm George," he said, grinning at his wife with admiring eyes. He slid them to Penelope as she released Finlay's hand and took his. "Sadly, I've been a Mr. Martell my entire life. Please don't tell my wife; for some ungodly reason, she still finds me fascinating."

"My friends call me Pen," Penelope said with a laugh.

She enjoyed the easy, harmless teasing between them. "I suppose I have you two to thank for our stay being so familiar. One would think we were in America, I see so many of us here."

"Heavens, don't tell the French that. We already have a bad reputation among them," George teased.

"They don't mind our American dollars though. When we first arrived, everything from bread to accommodations could be had for a song. We had a lovely little waterfront apartment for the longest time. You millionaires have ruined it all," Finlay said with a good-natured laugh to show she wasn't sore.

Sawyer snorted at some secret amusement, his eyes still closed as he lay back on his towel.

George shot him a harsh look, but Finlay laughed with a bit of self-deprecation. "Oh alright, yes, I suppose we aren't exactly paupers ourselves."

"They were living in the Hôtel de Platine for a while, at least until this spring," Estelle pointed out, her eyes impishly aglitter for some reason.

"Really? How lovely that must have been." Pen shielded her eyes and looked out toward the large structure in the distance, which was now completely painted a bright white.

"It wasn't called that at the time," Finlay said in a curt voice, all hints of hospitable *bon homie* disappearing. "Vera changed it when she purchased it."

That at least explained Estelle's impish look. She certainly liked to stir the pot.

"The platinum life isn't really for us," George said with a chuckle that rang a bit hollow. He reached out to squeeze his wife's hand reassuringly. "But we found our own little home here, didn't we, dear?"

Finlay forced a smile to her face, and she pulled her hand away to smooth a stray hair back. "It's sad, really. Vera wants to turn it into an escape for the privileged classes. Though, who am I to talk?"

"That said, who on this beach doesn't have enough kale for a hearty salad?" Sawyer said, his eyes still closed. One side of his mouth was hitched in amusement.

"But now Finlay and I can finally start a family," George said. That only seemed to upset Finlay, and she frowned in either irritation or resentment, her eyes boring into the hotel in the distance.

"Do all of you attend Mrs. Tynehook's parties?" Pen sensed the sudden cloud that appeared and decided to change topics. She was hoping one of them might elaborate on what Estelle had hinted at earlier, but had refused to elaborate on.

"Oh, no you don't!" Estelle said with an admonishing purse of the lips. "I told her she'd have to attend one of Vera's parties to find out why they're so popular, despite the unfortunate hostess."

"Yes, her snub of your friend, was appalling, even for Vera," Finlay said with a frown. "Still, it is rather a fun sport, attending her parties. It almost makes everything worthwhile." She looked off toward the Hôtel de Platine with a wistful expression, as though remembering the days when they lived there.

"Well then, I suppose I should hope she recovers enough from my snub to invite me again," Penelope said.

"Oh, she'll invite you. If there's one thing Vera likes, it's getting her way," Finlay spat.

"Well, it was nice to meet you all," Pen said, sensing a rant coming on. She didn't want her day at the shore ruined.

She made her goodbyes and walked away to rejoin her friends.

As she walked back, she pondered the conversation, as well as her official introduction to the Martells. She turned her head to get another look at them. The brief bit of wistful hope had disappeared from George's face, which was now hardened into consternation as he stared at his wife. That was most likely because Finlay now stared out at the Hôtel de Platine with fiery hatred in her eyes.

"Well, what did you learn?" Benny demanded as soon as Penelope returned to where Richard had finally set up their blanket and umbrellas. He had already gone into the water.

"It seems we should most definitely accept a party invitation from Vera Tynehook, should she be so inclined."

"You mean *another* invitation?" Lulu gave her a pointed look.

"Who told you?" Pen looked around in surprise.

"Pen, dove, do you honestly think I don't hear everything that happens, even all the way in France?" Benny said. "I, of course, told Lulu."

"Which I appreciate." Lulu turned to Pen. "You don't have to protect me, honey. I'm a big girl. This is hardly the first time I've had to sit out on something because of my race."

"Yes, Penelope, you do tend to coddle us so," Cousin Cordelia scolded.

"Well, pardon me for protecting the feelings of those I care about. At any rate, it seems my consideration for your feelings may result in a change of heart. I've been told you'll be included next time."

"In which case, we surely have to go," Lulu said with a devilish grin.

"Oh, I love accepting invitations out of spite," Benny said, wriggling his nose with wicked amusement.

"I suppose it's too much to ask that we simply relax and enjoy ourselves here?"

"Nonsense, dove, I'm having a grand time. And I fully intend to enjoy myself at one of these parties everyone is talking about."

"And here I was almost looking forward to it. Now, I'm not so sure. Do you two plan on behaving yourselves?"

"Absolutely not," Benny said, making Lulu and even Cousin Cordelia laugh.

Pen pursed her lips, but then joined them with a laugh of her own. "Oh heck, what harm could one little party do?"

"Don't jinx it, Penelope," Cousin Cordelia said with a frown.

"From what I hear, Mrs. Vera Tynehook jinxed it herself. And who knows? She may not even invite us at all, in which case this discussion is moot. Now then, I shall be forgetting about that woman and enjoying my swim, if you don't mind?"

CHAPTER THREE

After only a few hours, Penelope and her friends meandered back to their villa for a quick lunch and then on to a long siesta before dinner. The sun, sand, and water had succeeded in making them perfectly lackadaisical.

"This arrived for you, Mademoiselle," Irma greeted. She handed a crisp envelope to Penelope.

"That was quick." Pen noted it looked almost identical to Vera's first invitation. She opened it to find another request to attend a party that Friday evening, *all* present parties included this time.

"It's in the Hôtel de Platine."

"So she's finally opening it to guests?" Cousin Cordelia asked with avid delight. "I must confess I've been a bit curious about what it looks like inside. It's been closed the entire week we've been here."

"That hotel?"

Everyone turned to stare at Irma, who looked alarmed and incensed.

"Have you heard something about it?" Pen asked.

"I..." Irma suddenly realized all attention was directed her way and she quickly shook her head. "No. *Pardon*, Mademoiselle. I should return to cleaning." She quickly left.

"It seems the Martells aren't the only ones who have problems with that hotel," Pen mused.

"I know bad blood when I see it," Lulu said. "That *mademoiselle* was full of venom just now."

"Not only that, she was worried," Richard said.

"It's no surprise that if Vera Tynehook managed to become persona non grata among her fellow Americans, the sentiment would be doubly so with her staff. I doubt she treats them any better, and they do have a tendency to talk amongst one another," Penelope said.

Richard eyed Pen. "Are you sure you'd like to attend this party?"

"We all agreed to go," Benny quickly said, before she could answer. He plucked the invitation out of Penelope's hand lest she decide to rip that one up as well. "Vera must want to show off all the changes she's made to the hotel. I say we attend for that reason alone. By all the tattle I've heard, I wouldn't be surprised if she's turned it into the next Versailles. I, for one, plan on attending court."

"I'm sure the French love that comparison," Richard said in a wry tone.

"I wouldn't be surprised if Vera has actually said 'Let them eat cake.' One wonders if her head will still be attached by the end of the night."

"Benny!" Cousin Cordelia scolded.

"Apologies, dove."

"I suppose we should see what all the fuss is about," Pen said with a sigh. "Even if it's the last party of hers we attend."

The rush of excitement surrounding the invitation waned, and she dragged herself upstairs to the bedroom without stopping for a bite to eat, Richard following. She wanted nothing more than to bathe the salt and sand away, then sleep for hours.

In the hallway, right outside their bedroom door, they saw Irma wiping down one of the windows so ferociously, one would have thought it was her mortal enemy.

"Are you alright, Irma?"

She jumped in surprise, then exhaled with a quiet laugh. "*Je suis désolée,* I did not hear you."

"We didn't mean to sneak up on you." Pen tilted her head to consider her. "What is it about that hotel that bothers you so?"

"I..." She seemed ready to tell them, then thought better of it. "It is nothing, I did not mean to cause trouble."

"There's no trouble, Irma. We're just curious is all," Richard said.

After a pause, Irma sighed. "It is cursed. Strange things happen there."

Penelope and Richard stared for a beat, then eyed one another with uncertainty.

"People get injured, horribly sick, things appear and disappear, strange messages on the walls warning the workmen to stay away or face death." Irma quickly crossed herself, though Penelope hadn't seen any indication to date that she was Catholic. "There was a horrible accident. A man, he was very seriously injured just before you arrived. He fell from a ladder. He claims he was pushed but there was no one around. He will be out of work for weeks. Madame..." She glared and spat out the last name, "*Tyne-hook,* she refused to pay him. He had nearly completed the job, but not fully. How could he?"

"Really? That's terrible. Perhaps I can help him with some money?"

Irma flashed a smile and shook her head. "That is not necessary, but very kind of you. He is with his brother for now." The look of concern returned to her face. "I do not think you should go to the party. I believe something far worse is coming. That woman, she is tempting fate with her parties, and I don't want anything to happen to you."

"It's very kind of you to be so concerned." Pen hoped she didn't sound too patronizing. She wasn't a believer in superstition or curses. Good things happened, bad things happened, and none of it had to do with curses. "We'll be sure to take extra care."

Irma didn't bother pleading the issue. She simply shook her head and then gave one nod before returning to her cleaning.

Penelope eyed Richard again as they continued on to their bedroom. Once the door was closed she made sure to speak in a low voice.

"What are your thoughts about that? It does seem rather poor taste to have a party at the same hotel where a man was so seriously injured."

"I think we should be on the lookout for unseen spirits, maybe a black cat or two."

"Don't be glib, Richard," Pen lightly slapped him on the arm.

"Not being glib, just skeptical. I sympathize, of course. I think it more likely this fall from a ladder was an accident, at worst negligence."

"If he wanted to place the blame elsewhere, why say he was pushed by an unseen force? Why not choose a more likely excuse? Sabotage? Another's negligence?"

"Perhaps he really was spooked. With so much going on at that place, I could see that happening."

"And what about these other minor accidents, messages, and illnesses?"

"Accidents are par for the course during construction. I'd be surprised if there were *no* accidents. The illness was probably nothing more than the common cold, spread between people who work closely together. As for the messages, maybe it was a prank."

"Perhaps Benny was right, she simply wants to show off what has been done to the hotel so far. Maybe it's to fight these rumors of being cursed," Pen said with a small laugh. "At any rate, I'm exhausted, so I shall take my bath and hope I don't fall asleep in the tub. These afternoons are wearing on me."

"I'll rescue you if you do."

"I suppose I can allow you your detective hat for that bit of heroism," Pen teased with a grin.

"Luckily, neither of us has a current case to work on."

"As Cousin Cordelia said, don't jinx it, Richard."

CHAPTER FOUR

F riday night, the five of them were dressed to the nines. Penelope hired a car to convey them to the hotel. Before they even reached the front entrance, Pen noted that the driveway leading to the hotel had not only been extended, it was no longer the gravel path she'd seen in passing when they first arrived to Antibes. It had been paved over, which allowed for a smoother ride, but took away from the rustic charm. It looked less like a provincial villa and more like the luxurious commercial venture Mrs. Tynehook was aiming for. It seemed there were enough workers for hire who weren't susceptible to superstition.

The facade that Penelope had seen a glimpse of from a distance was completely different now. The old front doors made of sturdy, weather-beaten wood, had been painted a glossy black. The fixtures were no longer rusted iron, but some shiny new metal. The beautiful vines that had crept up the exterior walls over the decades had been ripped away. The newly painted white facade was practically blinding even in the moonlight.

"She's done an awful lot, it seems. We've only been here

a week, and it looks completely different," Cousin Cordelia remarked.

"Good heavens, it's a blight!"

"I would have thought you'd be a fool for modernity and luxury, Benny. Who knew you were so sentimental?"

"Not sentimental, dove, practical. This hotel is going to blind any beachgoer when it's done. The reflection alone will have this alabaster skin of mine freckling, the horror!"

"I'm afraid I agree with Benjamin. I preferred the hotel the way it was," Cousin Cordelia lamented.

"Let's be polite party guests and not freely offer our opinions on the matter, shall we? I know she hasn't made the best first impression, but we should all rise above—unless properly provoked. In which case, by all means, liberate your tongues. Something tells me, Mrs. Tynehook will easily invite it."

"Did you ever find out what had Irma so upset?" Lulu asked. Nothing ever slipped by her.

Penelope pursed her lips as they exited the car. "Since you don't want your feelings spared, apparently there is a curse on this hotel."

"*No!*"

"I beg your pardon?"

"You don't say...."

Cousin Cordelia, Lulu, and Benny all spoke at the same time. Only the latter seemed amused by the revelation.

"We can turn back now. We still have use of the car." She considered Cousin Cordelia and Lulu, who both looked uneasy. "Don't tell me you believe in that hokum?"

"What did she say exactly?" Lulu pressed.

"A workman had a fall from a ladder, is all," Richard said in that reassuring voice of his. "I'm sure it was simply to avoid seeming negligent at his job. She mentioned some other minor accidents and illnesses, all of which would be standard at any construction site. There are no curses."

"Ah, well," Cousin Cordelia seemed appeased by that explanation, particularly from someone with his sensibilities.

Lulu didn't look convinced. "This place is bad business, Pen. I'll attend Miss Vera's little party. I want to look the woman straight in her eye when I make an appearance. But I don't play when it comes to curses."

"Well, it's a good thing the only evil tonight might be Vera Tynehook," Pen said, hooking her arm through Lulu's and urging her on.

That earned her a small laugh and she felt Lulu relax next to her. It was silly to be so easily spooked by rumors and superstition. Now that Penelope had arrived at the party, she was once again curious to see what all the fuss was about. She could hear a jazzy piano tune wafting from inside.

The lobby, where the party was taking place, matched the lofty aims of the front facade. The floor was a polished pearl marble with an intricate mosaic pattern inset. The walls were white with crown and picture frame molding. Picture windows offered views to the back of the property, where Penelope could just make out the foliage of a garden. Further on, there was a landing above the cliffs leading to the sea shimmering in the moonlight. A set of large French doors allowed one access to the outside. There were sofas and armchairs all in black velvet fabric with brass hardware. Lamps situated on tables added warmth to the bright glow that already filled the space from the lighting above them. The large crystal chandeliers might as well have been taken straight from the Paris Opera. Pen shuddered, wondering why that particular venue—with an unfortunate history involving a chandelier—came to mind. Did this hotel have its own phantom lurking in the dark corners? Perhaps there *was* something to Lulu's unease.

What was soon to be the long front desk, done in wood so dark it might have been ebony, was to the right. It was covered in tablecloths and silver platters of hors d'oeuvres. Tiny croutons smeared with pâté, smoked salmon canapés, caviar with blinis, small onion tarts, and more all had Penelope's mouth-watering. On a larger table further on, the French pastries, petit fours, chocolates, and other sweet delicacies were even more tempting. Waiters in ties and vests also wandered the lobby holding trays of champagne, wine, or food.

A grand piano was to her left. The crowd was blocking the musician who filled the air with music that belied the idea the hotel might be cursed. On that same side, a bar had been erected to serve drinks.

There were enough guests already there to fill the lobby. Many of the faces, Pen instantly recognized even if only from a single glance at the beach. Her view of the guests was assaulted by the sudden appearance of Estelle. She was in a chic, red beaded dress that brought out the green in her eyes, and a red satin turban with a single black feather. She already had a cocktail in one hand.

"So you made it after all," she said with a merry laugh. Her eyes landed on Lulu and glittered with mischievous delight. "And this must be the infamous Lucille Simmons. Such a *colorful* addition to the party set here in Antibes, if I do say so myself. Estelle Summers," she greeted, holding out her free hand.

"It seems you already know who I am," Lulu said with a dry look as she lightly shook it.

Estelle seemed to find that amusing and laughed again.

After Lulu released her hand, she took hold of Penelope's. "Come, come, I'm going to introduce you to everyone. But first, a drink!"

Pen had no reason to protest, so she allowed herself to be dragged to the bar along with her friends. On the way, the others made their proper introductions to Estelle. Two bartenders in tuxedo vests, crisp white shirts, and black bow ties were making drinks. Pen instantly recognized one of them as the young man Lily had been enjoying a secret tryst with in the early morning. Perhaps she had helped get him this job.

"You simply must try tonight's signature drink. It's amaretto and grapefruit juice with a splash of champagne—surprisingly good."

"I suppose I'll have one of those."

"One Cagna for mademoiselle," Estelle said with a conspiratorial grin.

"Did you say...Cagna?" Richard asked, his brow furrowed in puzzlement.

The bartender's mouth twitched and he nodded. "*Oui*. In honor of Madame Tynehook," he said in accented English.

"Female dog?" Pen said, noting how Estelle's mouth was already twisted with barely constrained mirth. This must have been one of the things she'd been referencing when she told Pen the party would be worth it. As expected, the guests were making a sport out of teasing the hostess.

"I know, it's terrible, but fitting. We do the same at almost every party. There was a Cabra Balando at some point, then some vodka concoction called Korova." Pen knew enough of the Romance languages to know that the first was a goat of some kind. Her Russian was nonexistent but she could imagine it was yet another animal

31

reference, and not a complementary one. "Peter is usually the one to suggest the names—he offers Vera some grandiose translation to appease her pride. Blessedly, *Madame* Tynehook considers anything other than English unworthy of fluency. Even her French is barely intermediate. She holds certain views about the Italians, Spanish, Germans, really anyone save for the Brits and Americans. And even then, only above a certain class and bloodline."

"I'll have a Cagna, as well," Lulu instantly said, earning a look of admiration from Estelle. "I'm just sorry I missed the prior parties."

"Count me in too. I do love a drink created out of spite," Benny said.

"Oh, I think I like you two," Estelle said, giving them a saucy wink.

"I know it's in poor taste, but I'm curious. I'll have one as well," Cousin Cordelia said.

"I'll just have a whiskey, neat," Richard said with a sardonic look.

It seemed awfully petty, making fun of the hostess while she was completely unaware. Pen almost felt guilty for accepting the drink handed to her.

"I know what you're thinking," Estelle said with an exaggerated pout. "It is rather mean and childish. But you have yet to meet the woman in person."

"Perhaps I should get that out of the way first?" Pen hinted.

"I suppose, if you want something even more bitter than that drink."

Pen took a sip as she waited for her friends' drinks to be made. It was surprisingly good, like a sweet and refreshing burst of citrus in her mouth, only slightly bitter. Whoever had concocted it, probably hadn't thought it would be so palatable.

Before the final drink could be made, allowing them to leave and find Vera, Pen heard a voice that could only be applied to the woman herself. This was mostly due to the scathing words that voice was spitting.

"Really, Julia! I specifically asked they be served at the same time. Go and see to it!"

Estelle met Penelope's eyes with a look that said, "I told you so!"

"I suppose that's as fitting an introduction as any. Come, allow me to show you to our hostess."

Once they all had their drinks, Estelle led them in the direction of the voice that continued to utter disgruntled criticisms toward poor Julia, long after she'd disappeared to "see to it."

Vera Tynehook would have been described as pleasantly plump if she didn't have such a sour temperament. She was seated, with a small table next to her and an empty chair on the other side. There was a lofty, assessing expression permanently etched into her face, as though she was judging everything her eyes landed on and found it all wanting. That expression only deepened when she finally noticed Penelope and company approaching.

"Well, well, well, Miss Penelope Banks. It seems you've finally deigned to honor me with your presence." A shrewd look came to her gray eyes. "Now that you're here, there is something very particular I'd like to discuss with you."

"Is that so?" Pen arched an eyebrow in surprise. She hoped Mrs. Tynehook wasn't going to make a scene about declining her first invitation.

"Yes, it has to do with this curse supposedly plaguing my hotel."

CHAPTER FIVE

"I'm sorry?" Penelope said to Mrs. Tynehook.

"I said, there is something I would like to discuss with you." There was a note of exasperation in Vera Tynehook's voice as she repeated the statement.

"Yes, but you mentioned something about a curse?"

"Yes, but we can discuss the details of that at a later date. It's all nonsense of course. Foreigners are so easily susceptible to superstitions."

Pen refrained from commenting on that.

"Thankfully, I've finally managed to contract with people who at least have sensible minds. The renovations are back on schedule. However, there is another far more pressing matter I need to address."

"If it's about my turning down your prior invitation—"

'No, no, no, never mind that." Vera said waving her hand again, this time in irritation. Her eyes darted to Lulu behind Penelope and narrowed with disdain before she brought them back to Pen. "I wasn't aware of your...*situation*."

"Situation?"

Now, Vera looked perfectly vexed. Pen was beginning to understand why she wasn't anyone's favorite. She had an imperious nature about her, as though she expected the world to accommodate her, all while apparently reading her mind. Pen had no qualms about making her explain herself.

"As I said, never mind that. Now, sit. I have something else I would like to discuss with you."

"Perhaps we should be properly introduced first?" Pen said with a gracious smile. "I'm Penelope Banks, and this is—"

"Yes, I know who you are, Miss Banks," Vera said in a testy voice. "The Banks family name is known, even to those of us who hail from Chicago. Respectable enough to make up for how *eccentric* your mother was. I suppose even the most suspect origins can be cleansed with a connection to a good family name."

Pen felt her hackles rise. She had always been defensive when it came to her dearly departed mother. Richard placed a calming hand on the small of her back, lest the Cagna in her hand end up splattered all over the face of the woman the drink was named for.

Vera cast a dubious glance toward Estelle, who looked on with droll amusement, as though this was all playing out how she had expected. "I do miss the days when one needed letters of introduction and a calling card in order to be graced with an audience. California, of course, isn't one of the *newer* states to join the American Union. However, as far as I'm concerned anything west of St. Louis is still the frontier. Though, I suppose this retched moving pictures nonsense will soon change all that. As a businesswoman, I must pay attention to such things. For instance, I recently learned that Santa Barbara was once home to the largest movie studio before it packed up and moved to Hollywood. Flying A Studios? Are you familiar with it, Miss Summers?"

Penelope had the sense Vera was testing Estelle, who still looked perfectly unruffled as she answered. "I am. But as you know, *my* family is in oil."

"Hmm, yes, oil." Vera still met Estelle with a piercing look. It reminded Penelope of teachers who used a penetrating gaze to have students wondering whether they were right about the answer they had given, even when they knew it was correct. Now, she was sure Vera was testing Estelle, or at least probing her for some fault or weakness.

"I was just about to introduce my friends, Mrs. Tynehook," Penelope offered, hoping to quickly get through that formality and escape.

"My dear, if I wanted to meet them, I would have addressed them. I'm perfectly familiar with every member of your household. I make it a point to know every American that settles here in Antibes." She cast another speculative look Estelle's way. "No matter where they, or their *companion*, hail from." It seemed Vera didn't approve of Sawyer, either.

Vera's eyes wandered to Richard. "Good heavens, what's happened to your face, young man?"

Penelope knew Vera was focused on Richard's scar visible above his collar up to his ear and along his lower jaw. Once again, Richard pressed his hand into the small of Pen's back. She had no need to worry about his temper getting the best of him. He had every right to worry about hers.

"The war. I was a pilot. My plane didn't land in the usual manner," Richard said in a glib tone.

Vera shook her head. "That ghastly war. I've no idea

why we involved ourselves. Frankly, it's only fitting we be allowed to settle here after all we sacrificed for the French."

"Were you in the war, perchance?" Benny asked in an exaggerated tone of innocence.

Vera glared at him. "I suppose I shouldn't be surprised at such insolence from the likes of you, Mr. Davenport. Yes, yes, I know *all* about you, young man."

"Oh, do tell! I'm a glutton for gossip, especially when it's about *moi*."

Estelle and Lulu both snorted with soft laughter. Vera's nostrils flared so hard, Penelope thought her nose might fly off. Fortunately, a young woman appeared to defuse her ire.

The newest arrival looked to be in her early to mid twenties and had eyes the same shade of gray as Vera's. Penelope assumed this was the older, non-adopted daughter, Prynne. She had on a pretty, light purple dress that made her irises softer and lovelier than her mother's. Considering Estelle had said something about Vera favoring the beautiful Lily, Pen had expected her sister to be plain or homely. However, Prynne was pretty in a subtler way. Her face was kind, if transmitting a perpetual look of trepidation. Her dark hair was pulled back in a loose chignon. She was rather thin and quite pale for someone currently living on the Mediterranean. Pen imagined her mother kept a tight rein on her, forbidding any ventures to the sunny shore. She instantly felt bad for the girl.

"Here you are, Mother," Prynne said, handing her a plate filled with hors d'oeuvres. Her voice was even more lovely than she was. Hopefully, she would one day use it to bid her mother farewell.

"You must be Prynne," Penelope said, trying to capture her attention, which still dutifully focused on her mother, waiting for her to even acknowledge her.

Prynne's dark eyelashes flapped violently as she took the empty seat and looked up at Pen. "I...um, y-yes I am."

"Don't stutter, Prynne. It's unladylike." Vera snatched the plate from her daughter as she scolded her.

Prynne sighed in resignation.

Penelope clutched her glass tighter. "I see you aren't enjoying a Cagna? It was named in your honor, no?"

Estelle didn't bother biting back a conspiratorial smile.

"Temperance is a virtue, Miss Banks. I've no need to indulge in hard liquor all night. Everyone knows I enjoy exactly one cocktail named in my honor at ten and then again at midnight. Unlike some people, I don't enjoy getting sloppily drunk."

Everyone noted the way Vera's eyes bored into Estelle, who simply laughed before explaining. "I'm afraid Sawyer may have been a bit too into his cups last time. His mouth has a habit of getting him into trouble." She gave Vera a patronizing smile. "Not to worry Mrs. Tynehook. I made sure to properly spank him when we got home."

Vera's mouth turned down at the vulgar suggestion in Estelle's tone, which was reinforced with a cheeky wink. Prynne blushed at her side.

A waiter passed by with a tray of sweet delicacies. Prynne's eyes lit up and she reached to grab one.

"No, no, Prynne. You know how delicate your stomach is when it comes to rich or sugary food. I've had the chef prepare a small cup of tapioca for you."

The crestfallen look on Prynne's face, matched with the longing in her eyes as others snagged their own little tarts, sent another pang of sympathy through Penelope. It made her dislike Vera all the more. Though Pen longed for one herself, she refrained for Prynne's sake.

"Enough prattle. I want to speak to Miss Banks. Alone," Vera announced.

"I should really—"

"Miss Banks would be happy to speak to you," Benny interrupted. He gave Pen a pointed look, reminding her to tell him everything discussed, after the fact.

"I suppose I can spare a few minutes."

"Of course you can," Vera insisted.

"I'll show everyone around in the meantime," Estelle said, hooking her arms through Lulu's and Benny's.

Richard pulled closer to Pen's side. "Just give me a look if you need rescuing," he whispered in her ear. She could hear the hint of amusement in his voice at her situation.

Pen watched all of them stroll off, being led by the lively Estelle. She then took the chair that Prynne quickly ceded to her. Prynne made to walk off but was stopped by her mother.

"Not you, Prynne. Obviously, you can remain."

Prynne seemed more resigned than anything at the honor, looking out at the party with a forlorn expression.

Sitting that closely to Vera, Pen was slightly appalled to recognize the hint of lavender in the air. It was the same signature floral scent Penelope used as bath water, taken from her mother. The idea that Vera had the same tastes was offensive to her sensibilities.

"Now then, Miss Banks, I've been led to believe you are a private investigator?"

"I am, but I'm on vacation at the moment."

"All the same, I'd like to hire your services."

"I'm quite honored but, as I stated, I'm—"

"Money is no object...to a point, of course."

"I assume you already know that I don't need the money."

"Yes, I can see that quite clearly." Vera eyed her with a look of utter disapproval. "Money in the hands of willful young women is a dangerous thing. That's why my girls get nothing, not even at the usual age of twenty-five. Not that they need it. Lily will of course get a dowry of sorts once she's married at the end of the social season, and not a penny before then. The *earl* expects as much," Vera said, a smug look indicating that Penelope should be impressed by the match. "And I personally see to all of Prynne's needs, so she has no need for her own income. She's a sickly girl, you see. Has been since the day she was born, the poor dear. I don't dare let her go down to the shore. The sea is filthy and the sun is much too harsh in this part of the world. Lily has become as brown as a savage, though she's always had a bit of the wanton in her. It'll be a week of buttermilk baths before we head to England. Speaking of which, where is she, the little vixen?"

While Vera craned her neck to search for her younger daughter, Penelope chanced a glance up at Prynne. Vera had spoken as though she wasn't there. The only indication that Prynne took issue with this was a practiced look of serenity etched onto her face.

"May I ask why you wanted to hire my services? Perhaps I can be of some help, after all."

Vera drew her attention back to Penelope, the pinched look on her mouth indicating she hadn't set her eyes on her vixen of a daughter yet. From her vantage point, Penelope could see Lily conspiratorially chatting with her beau tending bar. It was probably for the best they were hidden from Vera's sight by the other party guests. Pen doubted Lily's mother would appreciate such an association, not when there was an earl waiting in the wings.

"Yes, yes, of course. Now that there are no prying ears

around, I can tell you. I'm sure you've heard the silly little rumors about this hotel?"

"The rumors?" Pen asked in such a way that encouraged Vera to explain further.

"What I spoke of just now, this supposed curse on the place? I assumed the French at least would have more common sense than to fall prey to such silly, superstitious drivel. Then again, these are the Mediterranean ilk, so it's no wonder; the Catholic influence at work. The Americans here are no better. Gossip runs amok among this set." She darted her eyes around the room. "They have no couth to speak of. Yes, I know I'm rather unpopular. A woman in business is always frowned upon. Men can be as ruthless as Scrooge and still gain respect. For a woman, all sorts of labels and insults are bandied about. I suppose I should have gone to rot when my husband died? Allowed the vultures who sent him into an early grave to have their way?"

"Of course not," Pen said. That was at least one thing they could agree on.

"It is quite obviously someone sabotaging the work being done here. Since that man fell from the ladder—his own negligence at work, mind you—others began quitting left and right. Even though I've managed to have a few things completed here and there—you've seen the lovely front entrance and drive—it isn't enough. Every day that goes by without completion is costing me a fortune!"

"And you want me to—?"

They were interrupted by Finlay accosting them, forcing her way through the crowd in the large lobby of the hotel. She was wearing a bright green satin gown with long matching gloves. Pen feared for a brief moment that she might actually pounce on Vera, like a lioness on a gazelle; or perhaps a sharply tusked boar in Vera's case.

"You painted over the mural? How *could* you?"

Everyone in the large foyer was silent, having taken a sudden interest in the confrontation.

"I painted that myself. It was when George and I were trying to..." Finlay couldn't finish the sentence, she was so distraught. Penelope could hazard a guess as to what Finlay and George were trying to do at the time, if what she witnessed on the beach was any indication.

Vera looked on with indifference. "It was an eyesore that didn't fit the present aesthetic. Feel free to repaint it at the home in which you *presently* abide."

"But it was special! It was—!"

"Finlay, darling, let's get you that drink you wanted," George interrupted in an appeasing voice, coming up to place an arm around her and guide her away. "Just one more won't hurt. How about another Cagna?"

"I don't want a drink! I want her...dead. Yes, I said it, *dead*! She brings nothing but misery."

"Yes, yes," he cooed, guiding her toward the bar, despite her protests.

Everyone stared at the couple as they walked away, then cast surreptitious glances toward the target of Finlay's rant. Vera still sported a placid expression, as though she'd been bored by the entire exchange. Eventually, the murmur of party chat, now most likely about the incident, resumed.

"I'm afraid the Martells are upset that I bought their precious hotel. But it can hardly be called theirs if they held no deed to the place, could it? Obviously, I had to oust them to prepare for renovations."

"And the mural?"

"A gaudy eyesore. It looked like something from a children's nursery. Certainly not fitting for a grand hotel. I've had to do quite a bit of transformation on this place, most of it very necessary. Thank goodness I arrived when I did. That mural aside, their awful taste in decor was reflected in the large suite my daughter and I relieved them of. Gaudy wallpaper, ill-advised paint schemes, terrible chintz curtains, all blessedly gone. I want everything pristine and white, as you see here in the foyer." She gestured to the large space around them.

"I see."

"Now then, since we have a bit of privacy, as I stated, I'd like you to discover who it is that is sabotaging the renovations of this hotel. And that isn't all. I'd like to hire you for a more personal matter." Mrs. Tynnehook, for once, looked concerned. "I fear that—"

"I'm afraid I won't be able to help you, Mrs. Tynehook."

"What? Why ever not?" She looked appalled.

"As I stated, I'm here on holiday. It really wouldn't make me a gracious hostess to my friends if I spent my time investigating, as you put it, simple negligence. My advice is to hold off on construction until you can create a safer environment for your workmen. Now then, I really should return to my friends. Thank you for the invitation."

Pen stood before Vera could utter another protest. She left her looking perfectly incensed, which was fine with Penelope. As she escaped, she could hear Vera take her ire out on her daughter.

"Don't just stand there gawking like a fool, Prynne. It's almost ten. Get me my drink."

Poor girl. Pen hoped her little act of defiance just now would influence Prynne into conducting a bit of defiance of her own. Hopefully sooner rather than later.

CHAPTER SIX

P enelope caught up with her friends, who were still gathered by Estelle. Sawyer was by her side now.

"She wanted to hire me to look into this supposed curse on the hotel and causing all these accidents," Pen said preemptively before they could ask. "Sorry to disappoint you with something so banal."

"Do you think there's a curse?" Estelle asked with a teasing grin.

"It wouldn't surprise me if even the devil himself had a bone to pick with that woman."

"Sawyer, you're awful," Estelle said, slapping his arm and laughing.

"What I am is thirsty," he said, his eyes looking past the group and toward the bar. "I think I'll get another drink."

Penelope followed his gaze, considering another drink of her own, once she finished her Cagna. Perhaps something lighter this time. She saw Finlay had pulled aside Lily's favorite bartender even though there was a growing crowd at the bar. She was angrily whispering something to him. He snapped something back to her, mostly in impatience before returning to take orders at the bar. Finlay looked stricken, staring after him in stunned silence before she stalked off, back to George's side. Perhaps she wasn't used to the help speaking back in such a manner.

Sawyer arrived at the bar and briefly said something to the couple, which earned him a frown from George. He smiled back, then cut in front of the line to order a drink from the same bartender with whom Finlay had exchanged angry words. Pen was surprised when, instead of taking the Cagna for himself, he walked it toward Finlay instead. George intervened, practically snatching it from him. Pen noted the hard glare he gave Sawyer before he turned around to hand it to his wife. Finlay was still too filled with shock and anger at her exchange with the bartender to notice the look that passed between them. She absently took the glass but didn't bother drinking.

Poor Prynne was helplessly waiting behind the crowd for her chance to order a Cagna for her mother. Sawyer noted her predicament and left the Martells to help part the crowd for her.

"Lily! Come here this instant!"

The sound of Vera's voice, filled with a heavy dose of admonishment, drew everyone's attention, including Penelope's. She searched for the source of Vera's vexation and found Lily laughing with Peter Compton, whom Pen recognized from the posters for his musicals. He was quite boldly flirting with Lily, who seemed rather agreeable to it, though he had to be almost fifteen years older than her. Still, he was quite handsome in person, and seemed particularly charming at that. Vera called for her a second time. Lily frowned, then sighed and trudged over to her mother, who most certainly hadn't been agreeable to the flirting. Pen watched as she received a dressing down.

Vera paused to call out to Peter. "Isn't it about time for you to get back to the piano? I didn't invite you to make advances on my daughter."

Penelope grimaced with secondhand embarrassment for all parties involved. Peter, however, simply grinned and made an exaggerated bow before sauntering toward the piano. Unfortunately, Prynne had just managed to get her mother's drink and stumbled into his path. The two of them collided, causing Prynne to start so viciously, she dropped the drink.

"Oh, I—!" Prynne looked mortified at the sound of the glass breaking.

"My apologies," Peter said, a sympathetic smile on his face as he placed a hand on her arm.

"Oh no, it was...it was all m-me..."

Penelope couldn't tell if Prynne was more flustered from the accident or his hand sliding up to her shoulder.

"Allow me to buy you another," Peter said with a grin, knowing full well the drinks were free.

"Oh, please no. I can—"

"I insist. The fault is mine, after all."

Pen thought for sure Prynne would melt from embarrassment or simply from being under the influence of Peter's charm. The poor girl probably hadn't had such a long interaction with a man in her life. Vera didn't seem like the sort of woman who would have allowed it.

"Here, just give her mine, for heaven's sake. No need to earn yourself a tongue-wagging for not bringing her drink right on the dot." Finlay interjected, the Cagna sloshing over the rim as she shoved it Prynne's way.

"Oh no, your glove and dress!" Prynne said, her concern for Finlay overshadowing the impatience of her demanding mother. Pen could see the fingers of Finlay's long glove and the front of her dress had dark stains from the spilled drink.

"I can easily clean my gloves and dress," Finlay said with a humorless smile. "Take the drink."

"Oh, I couldn't."

"Sure you could," Peter said, taking the drink with a wink of thanks to Finlay.

"Oh..." Prynne seemed positively torn by the gesture and only took the drink when Peter forced it into her hands. She blushed ferociously as she thanked him.

She hurried on, but was intercepted by her younger sister. Lily threw an arm across Prynne's shoulder and swung her around in the opposite direction.

"Or, you could stop jumping at Mother's every command and make her wait for once. Heaven forbid she get her drink a minute later than ten." Lily leaned in with a wicked grin, pulling her sister closer and taking the glass from her. She giggled and brought it closer to her lips. "Or I could take it myself."

"Lily, please," Prynne said, rescuing the drink from Lily and disentangling herself from her sister's clutches.

She quickly rushed to her mother, lest anyone else try to create an obstacle. Vera was conversing with Julia, who had returned from whatever small fire she'd been putting out. She cut the conversation short to accept the drink and set it down on the small table between Prynne and herself.

"Quite the theater our hostess inspires, doesn't she?" Sawyer mused, rejoining them with his own Cagna finally in his hand.

"By popular demand, my ivory-tickling services have been requested!" Peter's voice carried, and the entire room devoted their attention to him. Pen could feel the excited buzz of anticipation in the air.

"And now, the *piaz de resistance*," Estelle said with a small laugh. Her mischievous tone was enhanced by her deliberate mispronunciation of "pièce de résistance." Sawyer breathed out a cynical laugh and shook his head in disbelief.

"This is a little ditty, inspired by the lovely Lady Tynehook."

Vera seemed unamused by the false flattery. Her only reaction was to purse her lips with suspicious anticipation.

Peter tickled the keys with a jaunty tune that had everyone bouncing on their feet. Then, he began singing:

That Shakespeare sure could pen a play
And Wordsworth, yes he had his day
No one out-quips good ole Mae
But darling, what can I say?

The words elude me
Since you wooed me
It's very sad but true...
I haven't got the words to say just what I
    think of you

My heart goes silent as a mime
My brain can't even make a rhyme
My tongue's as twisted as a vine
Please darling, give me time

'Cause words elude me
Since you wooed me
I don't know what to do...
There are no words to let you know just what
    I think of you

The English language won't suffice
Perhaps the French have some advice
And though those Germans ain't so nice
Oh darling, I'd ask thrice

Yes, words elude me
Since you wooed me
I haven't got a clue...
Can't put my finger on the word for what I
   think of you

By that point, everyone was laughing and merrily singing along. The double meaning of the lyrics wasn't lost on anyone. Yes, they could be interpreted as a love song. But as applied to the "lovely Lady Tynehook," they had an altogether different meaning. Despite that, Penelope found herself admiring his wit.

She glanced over to see if Madame Tynehook was catching on. Vera's eyes were narrowed as though she was carefully considering the words in her head. She picked up her glass and began drinking her as yet untouched Cagna.

Next to her, Prynne's cheeks were violently pink. Though, it may have been what Estelle was currently leaning down to whisper in her ear as she stood between the two women. Pen had been so absorbed in the song, she hadn't noticed Estelle leave their little group to join that of the hostess.

Penelope returned her attention to Peter who repeated the chorus one more time, everyone in the room joining in. Even Cousin Cordelia sang along, spurred on by the others —and the finished Cagna in her hand—completely without shame.

Yes, words elude me
Since you wooed me
I haven't got a clue...
Can't put my finger on the word for—

The final part of the repeated chorus was interrupted by the combined sounds of a glass crashing to the ground and Prynne screaming. That put a discordant stop to the piano playing and singing. Every eye turned to look in Prynne's direction. Pen could see Vera convulsing in her chair, foam coming from her mouth. Time seemed to stand still as everyone stood frozen in shock until the convulsions finally ceased. Vera went perfectly rigid, then slumped in her chair.

Prynne, her face white with horror, ceased screaming long enough to say, "She's...*dead!*"

Then, she fainted, falling off her own chair and down to the floor.

CHAPTER SEVEN

"Prynne!" Lily rushed to her sister's side, sparing not so much as a glance at her mother who was equally unconscious. Though, it looked as though there would be no recovery for Vera.

"Stand back, everyone!" Peter shouted, leaping from his seat at the piano and rushing over. He kneeled on the floor next to Lily, gently releasing her grip on her sister. "I've got her, Lily."

"Do something!" Lily cried.

"Prynne," he said calmly, lifting her head and lightly tapping her cheeks.

Penelope heard her moan softly. That was enough to allow the collective breath that had been held by everyone in the room to be released. Instantly, the air was filled with animated chatter and cries of horror as people noted Prynne's mother dead right next to her. The questions began:

"What happened?"

"Is she really dead?"

"It looked like she was poisoned."

"Poison?!"

"The drinks are poisoned!"

"Everyone please be calm, there's no need to panic." This came from Richard, his voice loud, confident, yet reassuring. "I'm a detective with the New York Police Department. Now, to avoid interfering with the scene, if you could please gather on that side of the room, away from both Mrs. Tynehook and the bar."

He worked like a sheepdog, his arms spread wide as he walked back and forth, urging the people to the opposite side of the hotel lobby from where Vera's body still lay indelicately slumped in her chair. It had been a rather undignified death. Pen was certain Vera would have been more horrified than anyone at the manner in which she'd passed.

Finlay stood frozen in place, a look of shock on her face. This, naturally, had all eyes turned her way. There was accusation, some of it quite sympathetic, radiated in every gaze that landed on her.

"I..."

"She killed her!" Pen wasn't certain who uttered this.

"I-I didn't—"

"Don't say another word, darling," George insisted.

"I'll contact the police," Penelope said before the crowd of guests could get going again. She was well-versed in the panic that could ensue in the face of murder. She approached Lily.

"Where is the nearest phone?" she asked in a crisp enough tone to draw her attention away from her mother and sister.

"There is a working one in the office behind what is to be the front desk." She pointed to the long desk on one side of the lobby. It was presently covered in tablecloths to protect it from the trays of hors d'oeuvres atop it. Pen rushed over and around it to the door of the back office. It was locked. She briefly thought of picking it, but didn't have any pins in her hair to do the trick.

"Allow me," Richard said, noticing her dilemma. He made sure no one was inclined to escape through the front doors in his absence, then rounded the desk and used his body to force the door open. Pen flashed a smile and quickly entered, while he returned to guarding Vera's body and keeping the guests at bay.

It was a nice office, already furnished with a desk and wood cabinets for files. Along with the phone on the desk, there was a large open calendar book. Pen couldn't help scanning it as she picked up the phone to call for the police. Mostly because her eye was caught by her own name scribbled down in the notes section along the bottom for that week. Written next to her name was "Investigator" with a question mark. While she distractedly made the call, she casually (meddlesomely) flipped to the prior pages for the year, her eyes scanning everything else written, specifically in the notes area from weeks earlier:

Red hair?
Wisconsin connection?
Santa Barbara.

Penelope lost focus as she heard the operator and asked in French to be connected to the police. Once she had them on the line, she briefly explained that Vera Tynehook was dead, possibly poisoned. The police assured her someone would be sent to the hotel, and she hung up. After one last puzzled look at what was written in the notes of Vera's planner, she returned to the lobby, coming to Richard's side. She saw that Peter had succeeded in getting Prynne up and into a chair out of view of her mother.

"The police are on their way."

"Good. Now, we just have to keep everyone from fleeing in a panic."

"Or throwing more accusations around."

Both of them reflexively glanced to where George had Finlay huddled off to the side, separated from the other party guests. She was visibly shaking while he rubbed her bare arms to calm her down. The stains on her dress and gloves hadn't even dried yet. They were splashed across her like the scarlet letter dyed a dark green, the guilt evident to everyone.

"I know it seems as though Finlay is the obvious suspect, but..."

"But everyone saw her hand the glass to Prynne," Richard finished for her, in just as low a tone as she had used. "Why be so public about it?"

"Especially right after she quite openly wished Vera dead. It would be incredibly foolish to be that bold."

"Unless she was overcome with passion. Criminals rarely think straight or smart in the heat of the moment."

"But...poison? That would have involved some form of premeditation."

"True." Richard grabbed his chin and rubbed it.

"Also, how was she to know Prynne would drop her glass?"

"That was an interesting little interlude."

"Followed by plenty of opportunity for several others to intercept and slip the poison into her glass."

"I'm sure the police can count on you to remember exactly who, and in perfect detail."

"There was Peter. He was obviously no fan of Vera."

Now that Vera had been murdered, the song seemed more tawdry than amusing.

"Then there was Lily, who all but forced Prynne into a detour while in her clutches."

Richard nodded. No one could have missed that.

"And I saw Estelle standing by Vera while Peter was playing the piano. She leaned in to whisper something to Prynne. Julia was already there before the drink was brought. It would have been easy enough for either of them to slip something into Vera's drink then. She was too focused on figuring out if Peter was making fun of her with his song."

"So that's five people, if you include Prynne. Unless Vera wasn't the intended victim."

Penelope's eyes widened in surprise. "You mean Finlay? That would be George or Sawyer, who originally gave her the drink. I noticed a look that passed between them. George definitely takes issue with Sawyer. I have to wonder why. I also saw her and that bartender having heated words just prior to that. In fact, he's one who seems to be connected to Lily as well. I suspect she may have gotten him the job here tonight. I can't imagine what Finlay would have against him."

"Perhaps that is something you should tell the police." Penelope didn't miss the hint in his voice. By now, Richard knew better than to directly insist she leave investigations to the authorities.

"Yes, yes. It's just that when Vera asked me to investigate the problems with the renovations, she was about to say something else before I cut her off. Her exact words were 'I fear that—.' That's when I ended the conversation. What if she was trying to tell me she was afraid of someone?

Someone who was inclined to murder her? If only I'd allowed her to finish." Pen felt the guilt stab at her.

"Don't feel too terribly about it, my dear. It seems there is no shortage of people who, at best, aren't exactly saddened by her death."

Pen scanned the crowd. Prynne was still distraught, which was understandable. She had witnessed the death happen right next to her. Peter was still next to Prynne making sure she was alright. Next to them was Lily, who looked oddly pensive, as though she was wondering who had murdered her mother. Or perhaps wondering if she had been too obvious in poisoning the drink? Julia remained stone-faced, giving nothing away. Opposite them, Finlay had stopped shaking, but still looked aghast. George held onto her as though he feared letting her go would be akin to sending her right into the lion's den. Pen found Estelle with the larger group of guests, now next to Sawyer. When had she left Vera's side? She didn't seem at all upset, but that was her usual countenance.

The fact of the matter was all of them had access to that drink in one way or another. But which of them had poisoned it?

CHAPTER EIGHT

The air in the lobby had settled into a kind of restless boredom by the time the police inspector arrived, accompanied by several uniformed policemen. Even the sight of Vera's slumped body, still ignobly displayed in her chair, had lost its shock. As for Pen, she just wanted the police to take Vera away to give the woman some dignity in death. Even she deserved that much.

The inspector who entered was a pinch-faced man with a thin mustache and sharp eyes that scanned the room, casting a suspicious gaze on everyone. His eyes finally settled on Vera, slumped in her chair.

Everyone watched in silence as he strode over to her body. He studied her, fists on his hips. His head craned this way and that while he circled the scene, keeping a small distance between Vera, her chair, and the glass which had fallen a short enough distance to avoid breaking. He inhaled and straightened up, then spun on his feet to face the room.

"Je suis Inspector Cloutier," he began in French. "j'ai été chargé de—"

"Inspector Cloutier," Pen chanced interrupting. "Par-les-vous anglais?"

He gave her a withering look of disdain, then scanned the room. He seemed to accept that his audience was mostly American. After an exasperated sigh, he gave a quick nod.

"Of course I speak English," he said in accented French. "Now then, who was the individual making the phone call to the police?"

"That would be me, Inspector," Penelope answered.

He pursed his lips, as though he should have expected as much. "And you witnessed what happened here?"

"I think most people in the room witnessed her death, sadly. I suspect it was poisoning."

"That is for the investigation to determine," he said curtly. "I will interview you first, then everyone else until I have a picture of events. Please accompany me."

Penelope eyed Richard before following Inspector Cloutier down a hallway, far enough that they had some privacy.

"Please give me your name."

"Penelope Banks."

He wrote it down in a small notebook, then nodded. "You say you suspect poison? Why is that?"

"It seems most likely. She had a violent physical reaction before going completely still. I...well, I've seen the reaction to poison before."

He arched a brow. "Is that so?"

"Also, she had just finished most of her drink," Pen said, quickly shifting away from that detour.

"And who made the drink?"

"The bartender, of course. The one on the right, when facing the bar. I don't know his name."

"Hmm, and someone handled it in between?"

"Well, that's rather complicated."

"Complicated? How so?"

"Her daughter Prynne ordered the drink for her. However, before she could bring it to her mother, she bumped into another guest, and it fell to the floor. That's when..." Pen paused before continuing, knowing how guilty it would make Finlay look. "Finlay Martell offered hers instead. Mrs. Tynehook was rather impatient, you see."

"Finlay Martell, you say?" He wrote the name down in his book.

"Yes, but how could she have predicted that Prynne would drop her drink?"

"Many crimes are those of opportunity, Madame Banks."

"It's mademoiselle."

"My apologies. Now then, you say Prynne, the victim's daughter brought her the drink, and Finlay Martell offered her own. Did anyone else have access to the glass that you saw?"

"Quite a few people, I'm afraid." Pen explained the course of events, from the bartender to Estelle and Julia standing near Vera. By the end, Inspector Cloutier looked perfectly perplexed.

"If I did not know any better, I would have claimed a conspiracy."

That was a consideration Pen hadn't taken into account. She replayed the events in her head. Prynne's reaction had seemed genuine. What if it wasn't? And all those people... Did they all have poison? Or was it limited to one of them? None of them had been fond of Vera, but there were certainly degrees of dislike.

Then again, only one of them had actually threatened Vera's life.

"You have a thought, mademoiselle?"

Pen debated telling him, then decided it was only right he had all the facts. "You'll no doubt hear it from others, so I might as well tell you that Finlay did verbally attack Madame Tynehook earlier in the evening. She even wished her dead. Still, it would be rather audacious for her to then poison Vera so soon after, don't you think? Everyone saw her hand off her drink to Prynne to give to her mother. She would have known the suspicion would immediately fall on her."

"And yet, the threat was made and the drink was handed over. Do you know why she held such contempt for Madame Tynehook?"

"I'm not sure of the details. Finlay seemed upset about a mural in the hotel that had been painted over. The Martells used to reside here."

"Yes," he said, an unamused hum in his tone. "The *Hotel America* is well known in Antibes."

Pen had no response to that.

"*Alors*, I understand Madame Tynehook is—*was* now in ownership of the hotel. I suppose it will pass to the daughters. Something to look into."

Again, Penelope had no response. Was he looking at Prynne as a suspect? She couldn't imagine the timid young woman doing something that bold. The poor thing could barely say no to Vera. However, one never knew what final straw would cause even the most docile creature to go feral.

"And you, Mademoiselle Banks, your relationship to the deceased?"

"I don't have one."

"And yet you were invited to her party?"

"Only because I'm another wealthy American in Antibes. I'd never even met her in person before tonight."

"We shall see." Pen gave him a sideways look, wondering if he truly suspected her. At the very least, he was thorough, looking at even the most unlikely suspects. "Now then, please describe your own actions during the evening, only go back as far as your arrival at the party."

Pen told him everything from the moment she entered the hotel. If Inspector Cloutier was surprised by her attention to detail, he didn't show it.

"So you have no idea to what Madame Tynehook was referring, this 'I fear' situation?"

"No, I didn't give her a chance to finish."

"Why is that?"

"I knew she wanted to hire my services. I had no intention of accepting. I'm here on holiday."

"Your services?"

"I am a private investigator. Only in New York, where I'm from. I'm presently on holiday."

"So you claim." He considered her with suspicion. "You were resentful of the deceased as well, perhaps?"

"Not at all." Penelope realized he would eventually discover she'd declined Vera's first invitation to a party, but she was disinclined to air that business. After all, she certainly hadn't poisoned Vera's drink. "I've told you as much as I know, Inspector Cloutier. My friends and I have only been in Antibes for a week. That's hardly time to develop enough animosity toward a person to the point of murder."

He gave her a look of dry amusement. "You would be surprised, Mademoiselle. For now, I do believe I shall move on to the next person of interest. Unless there is any other relevant information you would care to provide?"

"You do know about the, ah, curse on the hotel?" Pen said, trying not to cringe with embarrassment.

"These little acts of mischief?" He said in a dismissive voice. "Yes, Madame Tynehook filed several complaints. A waste of police resources. Do you have reason to believe it's related?"

"No," she said.

"Was there anything else to add?"

Considering most of what she knew was based on hearsay and casual observation, Pen refrained from adding anything more. Surely others in attendance were better equipped to give him a fuller picture of Vera's life here in Antibes.

He walked her back into the lobby. Every eye was trained on her as they reappeared. Pen's gaze flitted over every person of interest she had mentioned to Inspector Cloutier. She wasn't surprised to find reflected back at her a mix of trepidation, suspicion, and piercing curiosity as to what she had told him.

"I should like to speak to a Prynne...Tynehook, is the last name, I presume?"

"She's still in shock." This came from Lily, standing next to her.

"I'm afraid she's in no condition to answer questions," Peter added.

"Our mother has been murdered, and Prynne has a delicate constitution."

Inspector Cloutier arched a brow. "Mademoiselle Lily, I presume? As your sister seems ill-equipped to answer questions," he gave Prynne an assessing look, "I shall speak to you instead."

A man in the crowd aired a protest. "What about those of us who had nothing to do with this? We should be allowed to return home."

Inspector Cloutier gave the group a considering look.

"*Oui*, I agree." In French, he instructed the other officers to get each person's name and contact information before allowing them to leave.

He switched to English to make the next announcement. "I have instructed these officers to take your name and information. I would like the following people to remain: Finlay Martell, George Martell, Sawyer Hendricks, Estelle Summers, Peter Compton, Prynne Tynehook, Lily Tynehook, Julia..." He looked up from the notepad with every name Penelope had mentioned. "I do not have a last name. The assistant to the deceased?"

"Julia Tuthill," Vera's former assistant said in a placid tone.

"*Oui*," Inspector Cloutier said, making note of her surname in his little book, before moving on to the next and last individual. "And the bartender who made the drink. I do not have a name..." He gave Penelope a questioning look, encouraging her to point him out.

Pen turned to scan the crowd, which was only about forty people in total. Still, the handsome young man didn't materialize in her view.

"I don't see him. He's gone."

CHAPTER NINE

The announcement that the bartender had disappeared caused a stir in the crowd. Most of the guests were either alarmed or surprised. At least a handful of faces showed a degree of relief, mostly at having the shadow of suspicion now falling completely on said bartender.

"Marc?" Lily said. "Surely, he's not a suspect. He just made the drink."

"You know this man personally?" Inspector Cloutier demanded.

Lily's face colored, but she shrugged with feigned nonchalance. "Only in passing. He's done some work on the renovations here. I must have heard one of the other workmen mention his name. I don't consort with the help, if that's what you are trying to insinuate." She couldn't help a quick dart of the eyes to Penelope as she said this, knowing full well she had seen Lily and Marc consorting quite flagrantly earlier in the week.

"His name is Marc Ravier," Julia announced in a placid tone. "I was in charge of hiring the staff for the party." She seemed to deliberately avoid looking Lily's way, not wanting to implicate her any further.

Penelope glanced at Finlay, who had recovered enough to maintain a facade of innocence. George still hovered nearby, his arm protectively around her waist. Pen slid her eyes to Estelle and Sawyer, who were equally poker-faced, a sliver of space between them as though they were facing this not as a couple but each on their own. They had both been on either end of the conveyor belt of suspects who had access to that drink.

"I see I will have to call in a search for this missing Marc Ravier," Inspector Cloutier said with irritation. "In the meantime, the rest of you will give your information to these officers, as well as anything you may have seen that was relevant. Those of you whose name I called will remain."

Penelope didn't miss the way most of those instructed to remain cast quick glances at each other. Was it due to a conspiracy, or simply curiosity as to which of them was the guilty party? Eventually, each glance slid right back to Penelope, trying to read her for clues as to what she had revealed to the inspector.

It was only a week into their stay in Antibes, and already Penelope's summer holiday was feeling rather chilly.

Penelope and her friends left the hotel after everyone else, other than those on the list of names instructed to remain there.

Inspector Cloutier had made the call to begin a search for the missing Marc, who had done himself no favors by disappearing before the police arrived.

Although the experience had been long and tiring, no one was in the mood to sleep by the time they returned to the villa.

"So, who do we suspect?" Benny asked as soon as they had all passed the threshold. He quickly gave Penelope and Richard hard looks. "And none of your talk about staying out of it. This is simply...conjecture."

Penelope wasn't surprised to see him head straight for the bar and pour himself something. After all, the party had been cut short, each of them getting, at most, only two drinks in.

"It had to have been that bartender, no?" Cousin Cordelia said, happily obliging him. "Why else would he have run off?"

"If it was that Miss Finlay, all I have to say is, she is one brazen *femme fatale*," Lulu said. Pen was surprised to sense a small hint of something approaching admiration in her tone. She joined Benny in a drink of her own, then sat on the large sofa next to him.

"Or just stupid and rash," Penelope said. She sank into one of the armchairs.

"I feel terrible for those two sisters. To lose their mother in such an awful way," Cousin Cordelia lamented.

"Unless of course they did the deed. I'm sure I wasn't the only one to notice that little tango of theirs before the poisoned chalice came to Madame Vera's lips," Benny said, primly bringing his own drink to his.

Pen felt a stab of guilt, remembering how she had hoped Prynne would find a way from beneath her mother's thumb. She certainly hadn't predicted something like this. Benny was right though, the question remained as to whether one of Vera's daughters had slipped the poison into the drink.

"We should focus on who had an obvious motive," Pen said.

Richard exhaled noticeably enough to express his opposition, then went over to pour himself a splash of whiskey before taking the armchair next to her. "I suppose a bit of harmless theorizing won't hurt, especially now that we've already given our official statements to the police."

Pen smiled at his indulging them.

"I'm sure I'm not the only one thinking perhaps Finlay might have done it," Cousin Cordelia said. She had nabbed a tiny splash of cognac for herself, "medicinal needs" and such.

"A bit too on the nose," Benny offered. "I don't like it. What fun is such an obvious candidate?"

"I don't think fun should be the operative word," Richard said.

"Oh, you know what I mean. Why her, when so many people had the opportunity? I noticed how Estelle sidled her way to the hostess's side in time to poison the drink. It almost makes me like her even more."

"But what would be her motive?" Richard asked.

"Surely you noticed the way Vera prodded her after she brought us over for introductions," Pen said.

"I also noticed how unbothered she seemed by that prodding."

"So, she puts on a good show," Pen replied, hearing how weak that argument was.

"That bartender sure skedaddled quickly enough. What do you make of that?" Lulu asked.

"The only explanation is that he wanted to avoid the authorities, surely," Cousin Cordelia said. "He knew his guilt would be discovered."

"People have a lot of reasons for not wanting to get involved with the police," Lulu replied.

"It probably makes sense to focus on anyone who had access to the drink after Finlay handed it to Prynne," Richard said.

"Inspector Cloutier did suggest there might have been a conspiracy involving all of them."

Everyone paused to consider that.

Lulu was the one to finally break the silence. "If so, it was a darn good show they put on."

"Equally guilty, equally innocent," Richard mused. "Pretty brilliant, bringing so many people together."

"Except they aren't all equally guilty, at least not on the face of it," Pen said. "Finlay was the one to openly threaten Vera and offer her drink to Prynne. By comparison, everyone else might as well be as innocent as a lamb. As you pointed out, we still don't know what Estelle's motive is, or that of several others, including Marc." Pen nibbled on her thumb as she shook her head. "No, I think this was the work of one of them, and I would bet anything that it wasn't Finlay. She was just...convenient. Unfortunately, that still leaves quite a few suspects."

"I suppose the police may have to focus on the murder weapon itself, the poison," Richard said, rubbing his chin in thought. "Not only that, but how the killer got it into Vera's glass."

CHAPTER TEN

The next morning, Penelope woke early as usual. The sun had just barely pierced the horizon when she slipped out of bed. This time, her escape didn't go unnoticed.

"Sneaking off again on your own, are you?" Richard said, blinking one eye open.

"Would you believe me if I said I simply wanted to explore Old Antibes before the city wakes?"

Richard sighed and sat up, leaning against the headboard. "No, and you'd think me a fool if I did."

"I could never."

"That's at least reassuring. So, care to tell me what you're really after?"

"Estelle. She likes to visit the beach early. I thought I might run into her."

"And do a little interrogating?"

"Aren't you curious as to what motive she might have?"

"I don't suspect she has much of one at all. There are several other far more likely candidates."

Pen settled back down on the edge of the bed.

"Speaking of interrogation, I've been dancing around Vera's not-so-subtle prodding of Estelle in my head. It was rather odd, don't you think? That business about Santa Barbara?"

"I don't like to speak ill of the dead, but Vera seemed a bit of a snob. Perhaps that was her way of showing her opinion of people from the, ah, frontier?" A dry smile appeared on Richard's mouth at the reference.

"Come now, Richard. Even you have to believe there was something more there. What if Estelle really isn't from Santa Barbara? What if she's an imposter? Maybe on the run for murder?"

"All the way to the French Riviera? Where she openly cavorts with other Americans?"

"If I was a criminal, I wouldn't mind cavorting around the Riviera. Besides, you know better than anyone, criminals aren't always the smartest people."

"Which does nothing to ease my mind about you doing your own bit of detective work, especially without me."

"If I promise not to accept any cocktails from her would it make you feel better?"

"What would make me feel better is going with you. I don't particularly like the way they all looked at you last night after you returned from your interview with Inspector Cloutier."

"You coming along wouldn't be obvious to Estelle at all," she retorted, her voice full of sarcasm.

"But it *would* be safe."

"Richard, by now I know how to handle these things in a delicate way, and I have yet to be permanently scathed."

He sighed and threw up his hands. "I'm not going to be the kind of husband who tells his wife what to do and what not to. Just remember, there is already an inspector on the case, so there is no need for you to put the screws on."

"Yes, darling."

"I expect to see you by breakfast, my dear."

"So much for not dictating my actions," she sassed with a laugh before popping up from the edge of the bed to get dressed.

"Breakfast!" Richard shouted after her when she disappeared into the bathroom to freshen up.

Penelope left the villa and wandered Old Antibes, quickly making her way down to the shore. She was disappointed to find that Estelle wasn't taking advantage of the early morning as she had before. Then again, murder was likely to interrupt one's usual routine.

Feeling rather peckish, Pen meandered back through Antibes on her way home. Berthe had bought sardines and anchovies at her request, and she was already savoring some on a bit of toast with butter. She had just turned a corner when she ran right into Lily, scurrying out from a small alleyway.

The young woman's bright blue eyes widened in surprise, then indignation. "What are you doing here? Following me?"

"No, I was just wandering Antibes. How are you, dear?"

Lily recovered, now meeting Penelope with narrowed eyes. "After you practically handed my sister and me over to that inspector on a platter?"

"I did no such thing." Pen arched a brow. "I also refrained from mentioning your little tête-à-tête with Marc earlier in the week."

Lily stiffened at the name. "He didn't do anything."

"Except run before the police arrived."

"He's just—he knew how it would look for him. A poor

French boy against wealthy Americans. And...he has a history."

"Trouble with the police?" Penelope guessed. "I'm sure it was nothing that would make anyone think he'd rise to the level of murder."

Lily coughed out a bitter laugh. "That's easy for you to say. The police wouldn't be so benevolent. It was a silly fight, that's all. Auguste, the man who owns the boulangerie he worked at, he didn't pay him his fair wage. So Marc, he... well, he got a bit physical. The coward called the police on him for a simple push. He wasn't even injured. It was an excuse not to pay him anything at all. And then, it was nearly impossible for Marc to find work elsewhere. You have no understanding of his family situation. His father was killed in the war, and they had *nothing* after that. He just got scared last night, is all. His mother and sister depend on his earnings. What he makes at that tiny grocery is pitiful. That's why I—" She stopped short before revealing too much of her connection with Marc.

"You got him the job last night serving as a bartender?"

Lily simply lifted her chin and met her under a hooded gaze, which answered the question. She probably knew where Marc was at that very moment. In fact, Pen might have caught the girl leaving him. She knew better than to question her about it. That would lead to nothing but silence.

"He should go to the police to explain everything you just said. It would make him look less guilty. He certainly had no reason to kill your mother, after all."

Lily blinked a few times, which gave Penelope pause. There was definitely more to this, enough to perhaps belie what Penelope had just suggested about his lack of motive.

She couldn't help but think of that small spat he'd had with Finlay.

"How are *you*, Lily?"

"I...I'm fine." There was a slight tremble in her bottom lip as she said it, which suggested she wasn't fine.

"I lost my own mother when I was about your age. It was heartbreaking."

Lily gave her a cynical look. "Then, your mother was nothing like mine."

"Most likely, but it *is* still a loss."

"Not really. Mother only adopted me for Prynne's sake after my *real* parents died. I was only five, old enough to be a companion." She coughed out a sharp laugh. "More like a doll to play with, keep her company, and see to her needs when Mother couldn't be bothered. It was only when I was older and men..." she sneered with contempt, "men began to show an interest in me that she saw what value I had beyond just, for all intents and purposes, a servant. Then I became a doll again, dressed and made up. Diets to make my waist a bit smaller. Dyes to make my hair a bit blonder. Classes to make everything about me a bit more cultured. I suppose I was more of a puppet than a doll, now that I think about it. Well, Mother got what she wanted out of it, didn't she?"

"That sounds awful."

"Yes," Lily sighed, then offered a humorless smile. "Prynne was the one good thing in my life, a sister. She's the only one who has ever cared about me. Even when she was so sick, we all thought..." She blinked away tears. "She still insisted that I be allowed to have a bit of fun on my own, go to the park, or parties, or something beyond sitting at her bedside to keep her company. I'd do anything for Prynne."

Including commit murder? Penelope wondered, but knew better than to ask.

"Was this trip to France in anticipation of your... upcoming nuptials? Perhaps your mother had a change of heart, wanted you to have a bit of enjoyment before you married."

"I would never assume that much generosity in her." Lily spat before frowning in puzzlement. "I don't know why we came here. Mother always hated climates that were too warm. She preferred it as cold as the blood that ran through her veins. I suppose it was that hotel. One good thing I can say about her is that she had a head for business, more so than even father."

"Estelle said something about you marrying an earl? That doesn't sound terrible," Penelope risked asking.

The look of disgust she was rewarded with was exactly what she was after. It opened the floodgates of Lily's potential motive. "He's old enough to be my father and a bully besides that! She couldn't wait to sell me off, especially now that Prynne hasn't died before her time as she always predicted. I thought I'd be free once I turned eighteen, but she made sure I still knew my place. Her little prize, her trophy. I should be *grateful* she rescued me from the orphanage I'd been left at when I was only five. I should be *grateful* to grow up in such *grand trappings. Grateful* to become a countess, live in some stuffy old manor far away from anything interesting at all." Lily coughed out a laugh. "When I at first said no, she threatened to throw me out into the street with nothing more than the clothes on my back, and perhaps not even that! Not that she ever gave me anything to begin with, not even a tiny allowance."

"I suppose you'll be breaking your engagement now?"

Lily wasn't stupid, and read right through that question.

"Prynne gets everything, as dear Mother has reminded me on many occasions. Thus, I had no reason to kill her." Lily glared at her, preempting Pen before she could make the next obvious conclusion. "But Prynne would have never poisoned our mother. She doesn't have it in her."

The usual sentiment of many a person who discovered they didn't know someone as well as they thought.

Lily breathed out a cynical laugh and fell against the wall. "Frankly, if she was going to do it, she would have done it long before now. I remember once when Prynne stood up to Mother, refusing some medicine that had been recommended by one of her *specialists*—quacks, is more like it. By then threatening to send me back to the orphanage stopped working to keep her compliant. I would have happily gone back at that point. It almost worked, then Mother cut off all my hair, down to the scalp."

Penelope gasped. Vera truly was a vile, vengeful woman.

Lily's frown of resentment turned into a smug smile. "I told everyone it had been a case of lice. Even Prynne had a laugh over how scandalized Mother had been. She never tried that again." Her smile faded. "Then Mother stopped using me as a bargaining tool and began using other means. One day she simply collapsed in the foyer. Too much sleeping powder to 'counter with the pain of a vengeful daughter who didn't appreciate all her sacrifices.' I didn't buy it for one moment, but Prynne was inconsolable."

Goodness, Penelope couldn't imagine living with a mother like that. Her own had encouraged her to think independently and often admired Pen's defiant ways.

"Prynne carried on as she always did, with a stiff upper lip, pliant and complacent once again. Honestly, a part of me wishes she *did* poison the wretched old—" Lily remembered herself and averted her gaze. She pushed away from the wall to walk away. "At any rate, I had no reason to kill her, and Prynne didn't have it in her. You should be looking at almost anyone else at that party."

Penelope wasn't about to let her go so easily. Not when she was already giving away information so freely. "Why did Peter agree to play at your mother's parties? Did she have something on him?"

Lily stopped walking and turned to Penelope with a glare. "Now you think he did it?"

"I can't imagine he willingly played for someone he so obviously loathed."

"It wasn't blackmail. Mother promised to back his next project if he came here to entertain as a way to stir up future interest in the hotel. So no, he had no reason to kill her," Lily snapped.

She was right, it pretty much eliminated the motive for him. Presumably, the funding for his next project wouldn't pay out until he'd served his time in Antibes, so to speak. Peter had every reason to want Vera alive.

"You're quite protective of him."

Lily narrowed her eyes. "What are you implying?"

"I just noticed how friendly you two were."

"You just leave him out of this. He would never do anything to hurt...Mother."

Penelope was certain Lily was about to say he would never hurt her. If there was something between Peter and Lily, that reinstated a motive for him.

"*Au revoir*, Mademoiselle Banks," Lily said, walking away in a saucy prance.

It really didn't matter, as Penelope had her answer. She also had a lot more suspicions. Did Peter really have feelings for Lily or was it something else? Did he know Lily wasn't going to inherit? Was Lily even telling the truth about that? If so, with Prynne in charge of Vera's fortune, Lily need not worry about being tossed out with only the clothes on her back. She also no longer had to marry the earl. Both created quite the motive for a beau.

As for Prynne, Pen hated to believe it, but she now had even more motive. There was the financial incentive, which was certainly enough on its own. Her life would also now be infinitely easier out from under her mother's control and manipulation.

Penelope pondered all of this, then reviewed the events of the prior night while she walked back to the villa. At least the morning hadn't been completely wasted.

"Bonjour, Mademoiselle," Irma greeted. "You have a guest, she is already with Monsieur Prescott and Madame Davies."

"A guest?" Who in heaven's name would be visiting at that hour of the day?

"*Oui*, a Mademoiselle Estelle Summers."

CHAPTER ELEVEN

P enelope asked Irma to have Berthe make a sardine sandwich for her, then rushed to the solarium. There, she found Estelle happily chatting away with Richard and Cousin Cordelia.

"Well, there she is!" Estelle sang, looking far more lively than the others at the table with her. "I was just apologizing to your beau and cousin for my dropping in so early. It's awfully rude of me, isn't it?"

"Nonsense, there is breakfast enough for us all," Cousin Cordelia said, eyeing Estelle with hungry curiosity. Pen knew full well what fare her cousin was after, and it wasn't bacon and toast.

"Off on another of your early morning jaunts?" Estelle asked as Penelope took a seat. She eyed Pen with twinkling eyes over her cup of coffee as she took a sip, as though she knew exactly why she had gone out on her little excursion.

"Like you, I like to explore the city before it gets crowded. If I'd known you were coming here I would have remained to greet you."

"I confess, it was a last-minute lark. Sawyer is always telling me I have no tact whatsoever." Estelle laughed gaily.

"Our house is always open to friends and acquaintances."

"Did you see anything interesting while out?" Richard asked, his brow rising ever so slightly at the open invitation.

Berthe brought her a plate of sardines on bread and Penelope added some butter, while everyone else looked on with varying expressions of disgust. She debated whether or not to mention her conversation with Lily, especially while Estelle was at the table. In the end, she decided it was worthwhile. One, Estelle probably knew everything mentioned already, as she had a nose for gossip. Two, perhaps it might engage Estelle in a little confessing herself.

"I ran into Lily." She took her first bite while they absorbed that information.

All three people at the table sat up straighter, leaning in closer to Penelope.

"Did you now?" Estelle asked, eyes aglitter once again. "Was she aimlessly wandering the streets of Antibes, mourning the loss of her dearly departed mother?" Her tone matched the skepticism reflected on the faces of everyone else at that notion.

"She seems to be taking it well," Pen said in a neutral tone after swallowing.

Estelle snorted. Richard tactfully sipped his coffee. Cousin Cordelia seemed pleased, accepting Pen's reassurance at face value.

"I thought I heard a familiar voice." Everyone turned to see Benny entering the solarium, his lips pursed with dismay at having potentially missed a good bit of gossip. He took a free chair across from Estelle. "What have you all been discussing in my absence?"

"The topic du jour, naturally. *Mademoiselle Banks* was just about to tell us about her encounter with Lily this morning."

"I say," he purred, pouring himself a cup of coffee. "By all means, dove, don't let me interrupt."

"It seems Marc, our missing bartender, has a wee criminal history. That's apparently why he fled. A small spat with his boss at a boulangerie, which became physical."

"Ohh," Cousin Cordelia said, eyes wide.

"To my understanding, no murder was involved. As for killing Vera, what would have been his motive?"

"Lily?" Estelle offered.

"Anyone who thinks that relationship is anything but a flirtation has never been a seventeen-year-old girl."

Estelle tilted her head to the side in acknowledgment.

"As for that particular seventeen-year-old, she did mention it's her sister who inherits everything. I'm sure the police will view that as a motive for poor Prynne."

"Prynne who will be easily manipulated into giving the lion's share of it away," Estelle said with a purse of the lips.

"She is rather a lamb," Benny said.

"And you are a lion, Benjamin Davenport." Once again, everyone turned to the entrance of the solarium, this time to find Lulu sauntering in. "Shame on you for not collecting me before coming down to get all the latest news." She sank into the chair next to him and poured herself a coffee.

"We were speculating on Lily's guilt," Estelle said.

"Or innocence," Penelope pointed out.

"Is that what we're doing?" Richard said, giving Pen a pointed look.

"Consider it a public service, dear boy," Benny said. "Pen here is a maestra at getting information the police otherwise wouldn't."

"I estimate by now they have gotten in touch with Mrs. Tynehook's lawyers to find out about any will. And I can't be sure but I would assume the police have access to Marc's police records as well," Richard said dryly.

"We can always count on you to be practical, darling," Penelope said.

"I live to serve, my dear."

"Adorable," Estelle said, her eyes dancing back and forth between the two.

"Speaking on getting information the police might not, I suppose I'll be the one gauche enough to ask, what was that business about Santa Barbara and movie studios and such?"

Estelle gave Penelope a keen look, her lips pursed with amusement. "You and I have more in common than I would have thought. That includes not bothering to be at all subtle in our information gathering."

Benny leaned in and met her with his brow so severely arched, it might as well have merged with the widow's peak of his hairline. "Then do tell, dove."

To everyone's surprise, Estelle laughed. She shrugged and waved a hand in nonchalance. "It was bound to be discovered at some point. Madame Tynehook somehow knew as soon as she set foot in Antibes. I'm not the real Estelle Summers."

She said it with such indifference that Penelope wasn't sure she'd heard correctly.

"So...you're *impersonating* her?"

"In effect," Estelle said with another shrug before casually sipping her coffee.

"What is it you *aren't* telling us?" Lulu posed, her eyes narrowed in assessment.

Estelle smirked. "My real name, for one. Can't have you slipping up, not as long as I'm still enjoying myself over here across the pond. There's really nothing nefarious about it. The *real* Estelle and I...came to an agreement. It's a long and involved tale."

"And we have all morning," Benny insisted.

She grinned, enjoying the intrigue she'd created. "I'm an actress, or at least wanted to be. I got my start at Flying A. Mostly, it's been one or two appearances in a film. Certainly not enough to make do. I'd been saving up money, trying to make my way to Hollywood for years when Estelle approached me. Who knew my big break would come from supplementing my income via house cleaning just to make enough kale to live? It seemed *daddums* didn't approve of the man the real Estelle wanted to marry. They had an idea of eloping, but she knew he would hunt her down and drag her right back home, followed quickly by an annulment. He'd bribed her with the option of escaping to France for a year instead, no doubt hoping she'd get over the fellow." Estelle leaned in. "But who said the *real* Estelle had to go? It isn't as though any of you society people knew who she was. Something about new money and such. If you saw us, you'd understand why she chose me. The resemblance is uncanny!"

"Except for the red hair," Pen said, remembering what was written in Vera's diary book. Her eyes fell to Estelle's arms, which only recently had been covered in a fine, almost invisible, fuzz of red hair.

Estelle followed her gaze and chuckled, running one hand up her perfectly smooth arm. "You almost had me that day. Sawyer keeps telling me not to be lazy about the hair color. It's just so tedious being a brunette. Why do you think I wear so many hats? But who am I to risk an all-expenses paid trip to the Riviera?"

"Indeed," Benny said lifting his glass to her.

"What happened when Vera discovered your secret?"

"*I* quickly learned that Vera eventually discovers everyone's secret. She liked...having a lien on everyone's free will, so to speak. Terribly ruthless woman."

"Did she have anything on Sawyer?" Pen asked.

Estelle considered it for a moment, then shrugged. "I'm not entirely sure."

Everyone at the table stared at her for a moment before Penelope spoke.

"But, you're his..."

Estelle smirked and quirked an eyebrow. "His what?"

"What are you two, exactly?"

Estelle rolled her eyes up to the side and grinned. "Call it...an arrangement."

"While unmarried? What exactly do you get out of it, my dear?" Cousin Cordelia asked with a perfect look of bewilderment on her face.

Benny deliberately cleared his throat and met Lulu with a smirk that she matched. Estelle laughed.

"I met him on the voyage here. We had abutting cabins on the ship from Boston. He could see right away I was no heiress. He suggested a partnership. He'd correct all my faux pas and I would...be his companion."

"So, he was the one who taught you how to fit in here, like a proper wealthy expat."

"Having him by my side has certainly been beneficial," Estelle said. "He's the youngest of four brothers in a family with money. But I'm hardly close enough to him to know *all* his secrets."

"What does he get out of the deal?"

Estelle gave Penelope a droll look. "Oh Pen, and here I thought you were a modern woman."

That certainly raised a few eyebrows at the table, most

notably Cousin Cordelia, who inhaled sharply and shook her head in judgment.

Pen decided to move on. "Why don't George and he get along? I noted a bit of contention between them last night."

There was a barely perceptible tightening of the lips before Estelle spoke. "I dare say you should ask them."

"Where is Sawyer from?"

Estelle breathed out an uncomfortable laugh. "Really, Penelope...I can see why you have solved a murder or two. You're as tenacious as a bulldog. Even the inspector wasn't as inquisitive."

Pen took a stab. "Wisconsin?"

A brief look of shock colored Estelle's gaze before she quickly snuffed it out, leaving nothing more than mild surprise. "How did you know that?"

"Because Vera seemed to know as well," Pen said in a considering tone. "She had something about it written down, along with your hair color, your *real* hair color."

Estelle frowned at that news. "Sawyer went to Marquette University in Wisconsin. I don't see how his four years in Milwaukee are relevant to anything. As for *moi*, I have nothing to hide, certainly nothing worth killing over."

"If it was discovered that you aren't the real Estelle Summers, I suspect this little holiday would come to an end," Richard pointed out.

"And I'd still be left better off than I was before. If you plan on using that as a motive, you'd be wrong. Even though Vera had discovered my..."

"Fraud?" Pen said, earning herself a brief glare from Estelle.

"Bit of subterfuge," she corrected. "Vera was interested in what could benefit Vera. And I'm certainly not above looking out for myself to do just that. At most she would have used that information as leverage, should I become useful to her. Why would I endanger that kind of windfall? Something that never came to fruition, mind you. As it was, we had a rather fun little dance. She liked to remind me of what blackmail she had on me, and I liked to pretend I didn't care. Besides, there were far more beneficial...*selections* at that party last night for her to chew on and spit out."

Before Penelope could ask another question, Estelle was out of her seat.

"I can see I'm going to have to keep my wits about me with you," she said to Penelope, though with a tinge of amusement rather than resentment. "Thank you for the morning fodder. Ta-ta!"

She trotted toward the entrance, all of them watching her go. Just before she exited she stopped and turned back to them, an enigmatic smile on her face.

"I almost forgot why I came. I did learn one tiny bit of news that happened overnight. The police found Marc Ravier and arrested him. It seems they found their murderer, after all."

With that, she left, leaving quite the wake of surprise after her.

CHAPTER TWELVE

"Leave it to Estelle to be the first to know about the arrest," Benny said after she'd gone. "So, do we think Marc is the guilty party?"

"It's highly unlikely unless one of two things is true," Richard began. "Either it actually was a conspiracy and he was in on it, or the real victim was Finlay."

"Surely not," Cousin Cordelia said.

"No..." Pen said, biting her thumb in thought. She stood up to pace, recalling the night before. "Sawyer was the one to take the drink. I don't think Marc knew he would hand it off to Finlay."

"Which means, unless he had some vendetta against Sawyer, Marc is the least likely suspect," Lulu said.

"So why did they arrest him?" Penelope asked.

"Perhaps it isn't related," Richard said.

"Or perhaps he was just convenient," Lulu offered.

Penelope considered that, her interest in his arrest officially piqued. "It has occurred to me that I failed to tell Inspector Cloutier about what I saw written in the calendar book in the office. Perhaps—"

"Perhaps you should use that as an excuse to go to the police station and—?"

"If you're going to say meddle, Richard, then please save yourself."

"I was *going* to say inquire, but meddle works just fine," he responded, the sides of his mouth quirked in amusement.

"I think it's a fine idea," Benny said.

Lulu snorted.

"So do I," Richard said, surprising everyone. He gave them a dry smile. "I don't think Marc is guilty of this, and if that's why they arrested him, it behooves us to rectify it. I *do* believe in justice."

"Well then," Penelope said, pleased they were aligned. "You and I should go, post haste. I'm sorry Benny, but too many of us will just create a circus."

"Oh, I have no desire to go with you. This is far too involved for my tastes. Besides, I trust you both to lasso us in when our services are needed."

"Don't you mean give us all the dirt?" Lulu teased.

"Is there a difference?"

Penelope breathed out a laugh and shook her head. "Let's go before Benny has a change of heart, dear."

"Yes," Richard said, quickly finishing his coffee.

The Commissariat de Police was abuzz with activity. Penelope wasn't sure if that was the standard state of things or if Vera's murder had contributed enough to make such a ripple. She stopped a police officer and asked him for Inspector Cloutier in French.

"*He is quite busy with the juge d'instruction,*" he replied, also in French.

"*Pardon? A judge? Has he been taken to court already?*"

"It's different here. He'd be a magistrate who is involved in the investigative portion of more serious murder inquiries." Penelope was surprised to hear Richard answer, but grateful, as the man she'd stopped was already moving on with impatience.

"How do you know that?"

Richard grimaced before answering. "You don't spend as much time as I did in Paris with Americans and Brits fresh from a war without watching them get into a bit of trouble. The men who made it through...well, let's just say there was a period of pressure releasing that didn't always present in the most admirable ways."

"I see." Pen was tactful enough to leave it at that. She was no stranger to the sometimes disagreeable ways of men. Not that women were without their own faults. "So what does this...*magistrate* do?"

"I'm no expert on the French system, but we can assume he's taken the lead on the case. If an arrest has been made for murder, he'd have been the one to sign off on it... and probably with good reason."

It took a while and a lot of American ingenuity, persistence, and meddling before they finally had an audience with Inspector Cloutier.

"Mademoiselle Banks, Monsieur Prescott, how can I help you?" He seemed rather irritated to see them, as though they were a potential thorn in his side.

"I just remembered something from last night that I thought might be helpful. However, I've heard you've already made an arrest? You found Marc Ravier rather quickly. That's very impressive."

She had been hoping to curry a bit of favor with flattery, but Inspector Cloutier seemed to take it as an insult. "We are very efficient at our job, Mademoiselle Banks."

"Naturally, I never doubted that for a second."

"You said you had further information?"

"Yes, though I suppose it's moot now. It seems Finlay was the intended victim, not Vera?" She phrased it as a question, hoping he would enlighten her. She underestimated his ability to remain frustratingly poker-faced and tight-lipped.

They were interrupted by another man in a suit, who approached the inspector with an air of command. He addressed him in French. *"Inspector, what is the delay?"*

At the meaningful look he gave Penelope and Richard, it was clear the man wanted to know who the two people with him were.

"Ah, this is Mademoiselle Penelope Banks and Detective Richard Prescott—he is from the New York Police."

The man's brow rose at the mention of both their names. "I am Gérard Travere, *juge d'instruction* in charge of this case. Inspector Cloutier has informed me that you witnessed the murder?"

"Oui, quite precisely," Inspector Cloutier said, eyeing Penelope.

"I do have a rather special ability to recall things I've seen, almost as though in a colorized movie." Penelope was hoping this would also be deemed valuable enough to avoid an instant dismissal.

"Alors, I would very much like to hear this version of events," M. Travere said.

Penelope was pleased, but taken aback at how things had shifted. She turned to Richard questioningly.

"Oui, oui, it might be helpful for you to come as well, detective."

They followed M. Travere into an office, rather than an interrogation room. There were three chairs, so Penelope and Richard took the two across from the *juge d'instruction* who sat behind a desk. Inspector Cloutier stood to his side, looking rather officious and resigned to this interruption in his case. Penelope told the judge everything she'd seen the night before, in even more detail than she'd related to the inspector. She included what she'd seen in the office.

"Very impressive, Mademoiselle Banks." M. Travere truly did look impressed. "We may need to speak to you again about what you witnessed, for further clarification."

"Of course," Pen said, noting the quick glance that passed between the two officials. What weren't they telling her?

"So, to reiterate, in the office you saw written, 'red hair,' 'Wisconsin Connection,' and 'Santa Barbara,' all with question marks?"

"Santa Barbara didn't have a question mark. I assumed that was in reference to Estelle Summers, or rather..." She realized their morning visit added new information to the story.

"Estelle Summers isn't the real name of the woman you may have interviewed last night," Richard finished for her.

"Oui, we do know that she has been impersonating the real Mademoiselle Summers. The information was freely imparted," Inspector Cloutier said.

Penelope and Richard glanced at each other in surprise. Perhaps "Estelle" truly did have nothing to hide.

Penelope continued. "The red hair may have been referencing her as well. I'm not sure if she also revealed to you that she's a natural redhead. As for Wisconsin, Estelle admitted Sawyer Hendricks went to Marquette in Milwaukee, Wisconsin. Perhaps the note in Vera's diary was referencing that? I'm not sure what she meant by 'connection' though."

"Hmm," M. Travere hummed, pondering that. He

glanced at Richard. "And you, monsieur? Would you like to add anything?"

"Mademoiselle Banks is the expert when it comes to remembering details. I was right next to her and saw the same series of events she did, though I never entered the office. Everyone mentioned had an opportunity to slip something into that drink."

"*Oui, oui,*" M. Travers said, leaning back and exhaling with frustration.

"But...you've made an arrest, haven't you? Obviously, you have reason to believe Marc Ravier slipped the poison into the drink. That is why you arrested him, isn't it? Are you still investigating?" Penelope asked.

He studied her for a moment, then glanced at Inspector Cloutier before turning back to them. "I suppose it is safe to reveal this information to you both. We have found traces of *two* different poisons in what was left in Madame Tynehook's glass. As such, we are looking for two suspects, not one."

CHAPTER THIRTEEN

P enelope and Richard both reacted at the same time to Gérard Travere's admission that there were two types of poison in Vera's glass.

"*Two* poisons?" Pen asked.

"*Oui*," M. Travere leaned over his desk with a stern expression. "I trust you will keep this information confidential. We do not want a gossip train running rampant through Antibes interfering with our case, and alerting our potential suspects."

"Of course," Pen said.

"Could it have been a concoction?" Richard asked. "Two poisons mixed together, simply to make sure the deed was done?"

M. Travere shook his head. "That would not make sense, as the two operate in different ways. It was arsenic and cyanide, enough of each to be fatal."

"It would have been the latter that killed her," Richard said. "Arsenic couldn't have worked that fast."

M. Travere nodded in agreement.

The news made an already complex murder investigation all the more complicated. It also explained why they were still investigating. They were looking for the second murderer.

"Why did you arrest Marc Ravier?"

Again the two men across from her glanced at one another. "That arrest is unrelated to the murders, at least at the moment. We received information regarding Monsieur Ravier's other possible criminal acts. The arrest was...in haste. In fact, he may soon be released."

Penelope interpreted that as a few police officers getting overzealous in the face of a murder investigation, arresting the one "convenient" young man who had fled the scene.

"So you don't suspect him of poisoning the drink?"

"He is not a primary suspect at present."

"But we are not dismissing him as such," Inspector Cloutier added.

"Was there anything else you think might be helpful toward our investigation?" M. Travere asked, a hint of dismissal in his voice.

"No, I think we've troubled you enough," Richard said, already rising from his seat. Pen realized she had no reason or excuse to remain so she reluctantly rose to leave as well. They said their goodbyes and left.

As they walked out of the Commissariat de Police, Pen pondered everything she'd learned. Marc had no doubt been arrested in relation to the "history" Lily had mentioned. He made an easy enough target.

Then there was Estelle, who seemed to have nothing to hide at all. She had so readily confessed to impersonating the real Estelle Summers to anyone who cared to listen.

With two types of poison, it was quite possible that both Vera and Finlay were the intended victims. Or, at the very least two people who wanted Vera dead. Pen couldn't shake the idea that that calendar book held some clue.

Estelle's "red hair" and "Santa Barbara" origins were no longer a puzzle or a secret. So, was it the Wisconsin connection that might have had someone panicking?

Once outside, she voiced her concerns with Richard. "Does it strike you as odd that Vera wrote 'Wisconsin Connection' rather than 'Milwaukee Connection?'"

"Not necessarily. Milwaukee is in Wisconsin, after all."

"Yes, but Sawyer's only connection is having gone to Marquette. So, why not put that? Or why not just Milwaukee, where the university is located?"

"Perhaps he's from another part of Wisconsin. It's hardly unusual for someone to go to a university in the same state in which they live. In fact, it's quite common."

"I suppose so." Richard had made a good point. So why had Estelle focused on his university? Was their relationship so casual that he'd only mentioned where he'd gone to school but not where he was originally from? "Why was she interested in Sawyer in the first place?"

"I'm sure the police will look into it now that you mentioned the notes from the diary," Richard hinted, reading her mind as usual.

But Penelope wasn't done, as something had just occurred to her. "Why did 'red hair' have a question mark but not Santa Barbara?" Penelope continued, ignoring that warning tone in his voice.

"Because Mrs. Tynehook had yet to discover Estelle's red hair?"

"Then why write it down in the first place? As far as she knew, Estelle was a brunette. What if it wasn't regarding Estelle at all?"

Richard stopped and turned to face her. "Are you just

99

conjuring up scenarios because you don't want to stop investigating this on your own?"

"That's awfully patronizing."

"I don't mean to be. You make a good point, but there's no reason to go poking around about it now. The police haven't arrested the wrong suspect, at least not for Vera's death. Justice isn't in danger of being ill-served."

"Can't I just be curious? Don't pretend you aren't as well."

Richard grinned. "Should I even mention the poor cat who suffered the consequences of too much curiosity?"

Penelope gave him a begrudging smile. "With you by my side, I might be a lucky kitty who remains unscathed."

Richard gave her a speculative look. "Do you plan on going to each suspect with a magnifying glass to see if they secretly have red hair?"

"Applesauce, I wouldn't be that intrusive," she said, happy he wasn't dismissing her interest in further investigating.

"So you suspect another secret redhead?"

"Possibly."

"Two problems."

"Two?"

"One, under a certain light, far too many people are secretly redheads. Even mine under a magnifying glass has a slight reddish hue."

Penelope thought about all the people she knew with hair colors ranging from strawberry blonde to dark chestnut. Even those outside that spectrum, like Richard's dark hair, had a hint of reddish tinge when inspected too closely and under the right light. "What's the second?"

"They may have dyed it, as Estelle did. Thus, making it impossible to tell one way or the other."

Penelope puffed out air, scowling at him. "You really know how to take the wind out of a gal's sails."

"Hopefully, so she can swim back to the shore where we are on a holiday?"

"I'm hardly in the mood for a swim in the Mediterranean right now," she muttered.

"Then perhaps—and I should preemptively kick myself for saying this—perhaps we should check in on our fellow expats, see how they are holding up in the wake of murder."

One side of Pen's mouth hitched up. "Should I bring a magnifying glass to hold up to their hair?"

"Let's not go quite that far," Richard said, wrapping one arm around her waist and walking her along once again. "I confess, I'm a bit more curious about all of this than I should be after that double poisoning business."

"It is odd. Then again, there was no shortage of people who weren't very fond of Vera."

"And Finlay? Who's to say she wasn't the target? How could the killer have known the glass would end up in Vera's hands?"

"That could put Marc back on the list for murder. What if he did know Sawyer was ordering the drink for her? We weren't close enough to have heard them, so maybe Sawyer said something that gave him a clue. I wish I knew what that argument between Marc and Finlay was about."

"There were also two people in between Marc and Finlay who had ownership of that glass at some point."

Penelope twisted to get a better look at him. "Sawyer and George? Why in heaven's name would they want Finlay dead?"

"Husbands are the usual suspects when it comes to murder. Even you know that, Penelope."

"I suppose it's a good thing we aren't yet married.

Heaven knows I've probably driven you to murderous thoughts enough times by now."

"Never, my dear," Richard said with a smile. It faded as he continued. "As for Sawyer, I'm not sure what motive he'd have. Perhaps that's your Wisconsin connection."

"But what *is* the connection?"

"Good question. Perhaps the whole thing was coordinated? They all seemed chummy enough back on the beach."

"And not so chummy at the party," Pen said. "So you think it was a conspiracy?"

"I think..." He stopped to consider it. "There were four acts in that play last night. Act one was Marc making the drink for Sawyer who was ordering it for Finlay."

"It was then intercepted by George, who then handed it off to her."

"Exactly."

"And act two would be the collision between Prynne and Peter."

"Which led right into act three."

"Finlay handing her glass to Prynne."

"And finally act four, the dance of Prynne with Peter, and then Lily."

"And possibly Estelle and Julia once the glass was in Vera's possession."

"Quite the performance, wouldn't you say?"

"We just have to determine who was acting and who wasn't," Pen said. "I don't think it would be appropriate to visit the Tynehook household so soon after the death of the matriarch."

"Even if one of them may very well be the murderer," Richard pointed out. "So the Martells then?"

"We may learn who wanted to kill her, if anyone."

"Or we may find out that she was the killer all along."

CHAPTER FOURTEEN

P enelope and Richard stopped to pick up a bouquet of flowers to bring to the Martell household. It took some time to decide on something that didn't seem inappropriately cheerful or even more inappropriately amorous. Pen decided on lavender as the safest choice. The flowers at least made the visit seem like a social call rather than a bit of sleuthing. After all, the couple had yet to formally visit the Martell household.

The Martells lived in a rather stately home as well. Theirs was not quite as modern or large as the villa Penelope and her friends had for the summer, but it was a very well-maintained estate from the post-Napoleonic period. It was the perfect place in which to raise a family. The couple definitely had money. Penelope wondered which of them had brought it into the marriage.

They were greeted by a housemaid who opened the door. They apparently didn't stand on formality either, not having a proper butler. That seemed to be a common theme in Antibes.

"Hello, we're here to visit the Martells," Penelope said, hefting the bouquet a bit higher to ease their way in.

"Are they expecting you?" She had a defined French accent.

"Well, er..." Penelope saw George bounding down the stairs behind the housemaid, looking rather spry. He noted the two visitors at his front door, first with surprise, then confusion. It quickly disappeared as he reverted to the charming host he would have been under normal circumstances. He strolled over to join them at the front door.

Penelope studied his dark hair, looking for signs of red. In the shade of the interior, it was impossible to tell.

"*Mademoiselle* Banks, is it? And *Detective* Prescott." There was a cheeky tone to the way he announced each of their names, as though he was taking a jab at both the French and the police.

"We thought we'd call on you to see how you and, more importantly, Finlay are doing."

"Hmm, I suppose she could do with a bit of company. You two don't seem like the usual vultures that circle for a bit of gossip to spread around. Come, come, she's back in her usual haunt." The housemaid pursed her lips, but stepped aside as he waived them in, then escorted them further into the house.

They continued through to a sunroom, which looked out onto a small garden. The walls were painted a bright green save for one. That was covered in wallpaper that had a pattern of matching bright green leaves against a dark green background. It gave the room a cozy, old-fashioned feel, like something out of a gothic, Victorian home, despite the cheerful sun rays that pierced the large picture windows looking onto a lovely garden.

Finlay was curled up in a chair next to a bookcase with

leather-bound books in various colors. One sat on the small table next to her that also held a glass of lemonade. She was barefoot but wore dainty white gloves and a simple shift dress hanging from her thin figure.

"Darling, look who's come to visit us."

Finlay turned, and Penelope nearly gasped at her appearance. She hadn't exactly been peaches and cream before, but it was as though she had aged twenty years overnight. Her blonde hair was even lighter, almost white, thinner, and more brittle. Her skin was blotchy, as though she had just come in from a bit of outdoor exercise.

"Please, have a seat." She gave them a wan smile and gestured to the chairs nearest her, picking up her glass to take a sip.

Penelope and Richard glanced at one another, wondering if this was still a good idea. Pen was the first to take a seat. They were already there, after all.

"We just stopped by to see how well you've recovered from last night," Penelope said, handing her the bouquet.

"Oh, what a rare treat! George, perhaps you can find a vase?"

"Of course, dear," he said, taking hold of the bouquet and trotting off.

"This is a lovely room," Penelope remarked, if only to be gracious before any hint of interrogating.

Finlay smiled as she looked around. "Yes, green is my favorite color. I wasn't too keen on this wallpaper at first, but George managed to persuade me. He suggested I put it in my bedroom as well. It has a certain old-fashioned appeal, don't you think?"

"It does," Pen agreed.

Finlay met them with a frank smile. "If you're here to

find out if I killed Vera, I am going to have to disappoint you."

"They've actually made an arrest. Marc Ravier, the young man who originally made the drink." Penelope saw no reason to reveal that his arrest was unrelated to Vera's death. Blessedly, neither did Richard, as he said nothing.

Penelope studied Finlay's reaction. She blinked in surprise and her mouth fell open as though to protest. She snapped it shut, then looked off to the side with an expression of pensive consternation. Finally, she shook her head and turned back to them.

"Impossible. Why would he poison the drink? It was meant for me."

"Yes, it was." Penelope gave her a pointed look.

Finlay smiled in an almost patronizing manner. "He wouldn't poison me, he certainly had no reason to. We didn't even know each other. They've obviously made a mistake. I shall have to call to rectify the matter."

"So you didn't know him at all?"

Finlay studied her for a moment before hesitantly answering. "Mostly from bartending one or another of Vera's parties, really only in passing."

"It's just that I saw you two arguing at some point last night."

Finlay's brow furrowed, as though she didn't recall, then she laughed it off. "The young man had made some inappropriate remarks, which I thought rather unprofessional of him. It was for his welfare more than anything. Vera wasn't the type to suffer such casual interaction with her guests."

So it wasn't just Lily with whom the boy flirted. Perhaps he'd been tempted by the sight of so many wealthy Americans, he thought he might try to beguile one for himself.

"But it seems the police have accused him of far more

sinister crimes?" Finlay said, a concerned expression on her face.

"He did run, after all."

"But *I* was the one to hand over the glass. There were quite a few suspects. Odd that they should pick him."

"I expect the police will be making another round of interviews again soon," Richard said, not without a degree of sympathy for Finlay's condition. "That might uncover a more likely candidate."

"And those of us who last held the glass are the most suspect." Finlay offered a weak smile and looked off to the side with a sigh. "Those poor girls. Though, who could blame them?"

"So you think it was Prynne or Lily?" Penelope asked.

Finlay turned back to them. "That's for the police to decide. However, having spent time with both of them, I don't see them doing it."

"I've learned almost anyone is capable of murder, given the right motivation," Richard said.

"Again, if you're asking if I did it. I'm afraid I will have to disappoint you."

They were interrupted by George's return. "Here we are! I had a devil of a time finding a vase," he announced, holding up one containing the bouquet of flowers. He set it down on the other side of the room.

"Goodness, where are my manners," Finlay said, instantly brightening up. She offered Penelope and Richard an apologetic smile. "I'm perfectly indecent. Please give me a moment to quickly change."

"Oh, don't bother on our—"

"Nonsense, I'm not even wearing shoes," Finlay said, dismissing Penelope's objections. She rose from her chair and turned to George. "Please have Julien make more lemonade for our guests."

"We should really—"

"That would be lovely," Penelope said, changing her mind. If Finlay was suddenly disposed to properly visit with them, she wasn't going to continue dissuading her. They might learn something useful.

"Why don't we move to the parlor, my dear," George said. "It would be more suitable for guests."

"Oh no, we've put you out too much already. There's no need to move," Penelope insisted.

"Yes, but surely—"

"Nonsense, George, there's such a lovely light in this room this time of day. Much better than the parlor," Finlay said. "You two stay right there. George, be a dear and get those lemonades?"

"Of course," he said, flashing a tight smile. He left to request the lemonade and Finlay left to change into something more appropriate for visitors.

"This is leading nowhere, I hope you realize," Richard said once they were gone. "She knows nothing and she'll only continue to insist on her innocence."

"Then we'll just visit. We always meant to get to know our fellow expats while we were here. What better couple to begin with than the Martells?"

"I think I'd prefer the Mediterranean."

"Don't be a rude guest, dear," Pen said with a pert smile.

George returned with three glasses of lemonade on a tray. He set it down on the small table between the four chairs. "Here we are. Julien makes a fantastic lemonade." He grinned and winked. "Happy to add a splash of something stronger, if you care for it. I always take mine with a bit of bourbon. Finlay prefers gin. I, personally, never touch the stuff."

Both Pen and Richard declined.

George sat back in his chair and sipped. Penelope thought he seemed awfully chipper for someone whose wife was so visibly ailing, even beyond the emotional toll from the prior night.

"Finlay seems to have taken Vera's murder rather hard. I suppose she didn't get much sleep last night?"

George grimaced at the reminder. "Yes, she's...well she hasn't been well since Vera bought the hotel. You saw last night how upset she was about it all. I half expected the police to arrest her on the spot."

Penelope frowned with disapproval at his frank admission.

"Not that I would have wished such a thing, mind you," he quickly added. He frowned in contemplation. "Still, it was rather odd, her offering up her drink like that. I know she dotes on Prynne and Lily, one can't help but feel sorry for the poor girls. Still, I wouldn't have thought Finlay would lift even a pinky to benefit Vera."

Unless it was to poison her. Penelope could almost hear the accusation in his voice. Perhaps that was her imagination.

Finlay returned wearing a pretty sundress that she practically swam in. Once upon a time, it would have framed a pretty figure. Now, it looked like a frock on a hanger, though it went well with her matching white gloves and shoes. Still, its wearer looked a tiny bit more cheerful at having company.

"You really didn't have to change on our account," Pen said, mostly to be polite.

Finlay simply flashed a smile as she sat down. She

picked up her lemonade to take a long, satisfying sip before responding. "I really shouldn't be so casual in the company of guests, especially those bearing flowers."

"I'd say today of all days, you might have an excuse for not wanting to dress up," Richard said.

"Yes, I do hate that our first real visit with you is under such a cloud," she said as she stared past them through the windows, lazily swirling her lemonade in her hand. "I normally like to make it to the garden at least once a day; a chance to enjoy fresh flowers. The lavender you've brought is lovely, of course. This view is why I love sitting in this part of the house. There is something quite enjoyable about looking at pretty blooms, if only from afar. Don't you just love how our peonies are surviving the summer?"

Penelope and Richard dutifully turned to admire the peonies. Even with most of the flowers past their bloom, it was lovely. After a tactful period of observation, they turned back to see Finlay smiling. She turned to George and reached out for his hand. "As much as I miss the hotel, George was right about us buying our own home. A hotel is no place to raise children. Perhaps when this is all over, we'll get lucky."

"Of course we will, darling," George said, his voice sincere as he took her hand. "Rest and relaxation is all you need. They say that is when it often happens."

Finlay lowered her eyelashes. "Sometimes, I feel as though I'm being punished for—"

George quickly interrupted her. "You aren't being punished at all. These things just need time to happen. Now that we have this house, surely it will."

"Of course," Finlay said, pulling her hand back.

Penelope and Richard glanced at one another, feeling as though they were intruding on something private. Although she was curious as to what Finlay had to feel guilty about, Pen was relieved when she focused more on her lemonade than any discussion of children, or lack thereof. She was sympathetic, naturally. The heartbreak of not having a family when one so desperately wanted one was incomparable. It was the kind of thing that could devastate a marriage. But Finlay and George seemed to be weathering it with a united front. She wondered how long that would last.

"This really is refreshing during the summer months," Finlay said, setting her glass down after a long sip. She cast a conspiratorial smile George's way. "Though I wouldn't mind a splash of something to go with it as usual."

"Are you sure, darling?" He had a wrinkle in his brow.

"Yes, yes, no coddling from you, now," she replied with a smile.

George nodded and took her glass, then disappeared through the door.

"He really has been such a rock for me through all of this. And to think, my parents didn't want me to marry him. He was the one to suggest we escape to Antibes." She laughed lightly. "At any rate, the weather is certainly more lovely year-round. I thought I'd miss the long, snowy northern winters. Now, I wonder why I didn't come here sooner!"

George returned, gliding in like a prince who'd slayed the dragon as he presented Finlay with her gin-infused lemonade.

Finlay took a long sip and hummed in appreciation. "The doctor says I shouldn't drink, but I feel today of all days warrants it," she said, giving Pen and Richard a guilty smile before she took another long sip.

George looked on with mild concern before satisfying himself that she could handle the bit of gin he'd put in her drink. He turned to Penelope and Richard. "Now then, I must confess, I've heard the most fascinating rumors about you."

"No doubt from Estelle," Finlay said with a small titter.

"Yes," George said with a sigh. "She is a swell gal, but at the same time a terrible gossip. No doubt she's told you plenty about us?"

"My brief interaction with her was mostly spent persuading me to accept Mrs. Tynehook's next invitation to a party."

"Yes, Peter's always been good for a laugh." George guffawed before remembering how the last party had ended. "Well, I suppose he'll be happy, at any rate. Obviously, that woman had something she was holding over his head to get him to play—"

"Now, now, no gossip, darling," Finlay said with a censuring smile before taking another long sip of lemonade.

They obviously didn't know about Peter's agreement with Vera that Lily had told her about earlier.

"I spoke with Lily this morning," Pen said.

"You stopped to see the Tynehooks?" Finlay asked in surprise.

"What did she have to say?" George asked, leaning in with tactless interest, despite Finlay's caution about gossip.

"She was rather upset about Marc being arrested. I do believe she was sweet on him."

"Arrested, you say? Well, all the better that was a passing fling," George replied with a snort before sipping his drink. "Though, who knows? Perhaps they conspired to do Vera in."

"George," Finlay scolded.

"Let's not pretend the woman was a saint now that she's dead, darling. Lily had every reason to—"

"Oh...oh, my...."

George wasn't the only one to suddenly shift his attention to Finlay at her interruption. She had a hand to her head and laughed softly before swooning in her chair. "Darling, just how much gin did you put in my...?"

Before she could finish, Finlay dropped the mostly empty glass and slumped in her chair. George instantly jumped from his seat and leaped toward her.

"Finlay!" He pulled her into a cradle and patted her cheeks, trying to get her to open her eyes.

Penelope could already tell Finlay wasn't inclined to wake up. She was practically a rag doll in her husband's arms.

Richard rushed over to help, checking her wrist for a pulse. George continued to shake her, becoming more and more violent about it.

The doorbell rang, but no one in the room paid any attention to it. Pen gripped her glass of lemonade like a vice, willing Finlay to open her eyes. Richard continued to press his fingers into her wrist, then her neck, a grim look on his face. George was nearly hysterical, shouting Finlay's name over and over.

"What is happening here?"

Penelope swiveled her head to see Inspector Cloutier and Gérard Travere standing in the doorway behind the housemaid who looked absolutely horrified at the scene before them. Pen had only a moment to wonder what they were doing there before she saw Richard pulling his hand away from Finlay's neck.

"I'm afraid Mrs. Martell is dead."

CHAPTER FIFTEEN

George went from hysterical to rabid at the announcement that Finlay was dead.

"No! No, it can't be! Finlay, wake up! Wake up, darling!"

"Monsieur Martell!" M. Travere shouted to get his attention.

Inspector Cloutier rushed over to pull him away from his wife. Richard had to help him just to get him to release her. The two of them forced him back into his chair. All of them nearly slipped on the small remainder of the lemonade that had splashed across the tile floor from her broken glass.

M. Travere walked over, making sure to keep a wide berth around the scene so as not to contaminate it. Penelope looked at the glass in her hand and quickly set it down on the table before her. She pushed her chair back and stood, taking several steps away. He caught her eye, while Richard and the inspector still wrestled with George.

"What happened?" M. Travere asked Pen.

"I...I'm not sure." She had a good idea. After all, Finlay

had pretty much hinted at it. Her eyes slid to George who had finally settled onto the floor, moaning at his loss.

Inspector Cloutier let go of him, and after making sure George was firmly situated, Richard did as well.

"What are you doing here?" Pen finally asked.

M. Travere and Inspector Cloutier eyed one another before the former spoke. "We came to make an arrest."

Penelope's brow furrowed in puzzlement, wondering how they had learned about Finlay's death so quickly. Then, she realized he was referring to Vera's murder. Which was oddly similar to Finlay's.

"I must ask that everyone step out of the room," M. Travere demanded. His eyes bored into George. "You as well, monsieur."

Something in his voice must have struck a chord of rational self-preservation in George's head because his eyes suddenly snapped to the judge, and widened. "I didn't kill her!"

M. Travere ignored him and gestured for everyone to leave and enter the parlor. Once there, he turned to Penelope and Richard. "Please relate everything that happened, beginning with your reason for being here."

Richard answered. "We came to visit the Martells, purely for social purposes. Mr. Martell escorted us here to the sunroom where Mrs. Martell was. She invited us to join her, so Miss Banks and I took the two chairs across from her, and Mr. Martell sat in the one to her side. At some point, Mrs. Martell excused herself to change into the dress and shoes she is wearing now—she'd been in a more casual dress and barefoot prior to that—and asked Mr. Martell to bring us some lemonade. She already had a glass." Richard paused, realizing the next series of events were quite possibly when the crime had happened. "She had been sipping her glass before she left to change. Mr. Martell asked if we would like a splash of something with ours, bourbon or gin. Miss Banks and I declined. Mrs. Martell asked him to add a dash of gin to hers. After asking if she was sure, he took her glass away and brought it back, presumably with the gin added. We continued to visit until Mrs. Martell became faint. She...inquired as to how much gin Mr. Martell had put into her glass before she collapsed."

"Are you suggesting I poisoned my own wife?" George shot up in protest.

"Monsieur Martell, sit down!" M. Travere ordered.

George remained standing as he glared at Richard. "I didn't kill her. Why would I?"

Why indeed? Penelope pondered the possible motives and couldn't land on one. Still, the fact was that he'd been the one to take her drink away and come back with it. Before that, Finlay had been drinking it without issue.

Pen frowned as she considered that, something not quite fitting. "This was different from Mrs. Tynehook's murder. I don't think it was the same poison that killed her."

"My fiancée is right. This wasn't cyanide. The symptoms are all wrong. That was a violent death; this was peaceful. And arsenic wouldn't have worked so quickly."

Everyone turned to George, as though hoping he would provide an answer. He understandably became defensive again. This time, he at least did so in a rational manner.

"I'm not saying another word except to state that I didn't kill my wife. I have no idea how, or what killed her, but I had no hand in it."

M. Travere turned to Penelope and Richard. "Was there an opportunity for anyone else to have poisoned Madame Martell's drink?"

"Only if it was put in before we arrived."

The inspector and judge once again looked to George, now with expressions of consternation.

"You came here to arrest someone," George said, a spark of inspiration coming to him. "Was it Finlay? She was the one who handed the drink to Prynne to give to her mother. It was her, wasn't it? You were going to arrest her. Perhaps she knew and decided to do something drastic. She could have poisoned her own drink at any time!"

Inspector Cloutier sneered with disdain. Even M. Travere looked on with skepticism and disapproval. George had so easily shifted the blame to his deceased wife, who wasn't even cold yet.

"Monsieur Martell, we are going to take you for questioning. We will arrest you if you don't come willingly."

"But I—" George snapped his mouth shut. He lifted his chin, glared at everyone in the room, then nodded.

"Very good. Inspector Cloutier, please call to have some men come and secure this scene. You are to question the staff and these two more thoroughly." He pointed to Penelope and Richard. "I shall take in Monsieur Martell myself."

"Mademoiselle," Inspector Cloutier said, getting the housemaid's attention. Her pale face and wide eyes still showed the signs of shock. "Please gather all the staff and bring them into the parlor we passed earlier."

"*Oui, monsieur.*" She couldn't escape fast enough.

Penelope and Richard had a few minutes to themselves in the parlor as the housemaid went to fetch the rest of the staff and Inspector Cloutier called for more police to come.

"Do you suppose there is something to what George said?" Penelope asked Richard. "I know it was awful of him and is probably nothing more than an attempt to take the blame off himself, but..."

"It is something to consider," Richard said, scratching

his jaw. "There was that moment when we were turned to look at the garden. But where is the vial or bottle in which she brought the poison?"

"Perhaps she put it in before we arrived?"

"She'd been sipping the entire time we were with her. It would have to be something slow-acting."

"She could have put it in the gin. George said he never touched the stuff."

"I'm sure the police will test it. But that only begs the question of...why?"

Penelope nibbled her thumb in thought before answering. "Perhaps, like George said, she knew the police would eventually arrest her. And she didn't appear to be in the pink of health. I wonder what was ailing her."

"Sadly, an autopsy may answer that."

"Or her doctor. Finlay mentioned something about her doctor cautioning her against alcohol. Surely, he would know what her affliction was. Was it something dire enough that suicide seemed like an easier way out?"

"This theory of suicide is ignoring one very important thing."

"What's that?"

Richard stared at her. "As I stated earlier, Finlay all but pointed the finger at George. Why suggest he had put too much gin—or something more deadly—in her drink if she already knew it contained enough of this mystery poison to kill her?"

"Perhaps that was by design too?" Pen offered.

"In which case, the real question is: why did Finlay try to frame her husband for murder?"

CHAPTER SIXTEEN

The staff of the Martell household was now in the parlor with Penelope and Richard. They consisted only of the housemaid, a cook, and a gardener.

Inspector Cloutier began his re-questioning of Penelope and Richard, each separately. He began with Richard. That left Penelope with the staff.

"I'm sure this must be a shock to you all," Penelope said to the three others in the parlor. She was still shaken over the death, even though it hadn't been nearly as disturbing as Vera's.

The housemaid, Sara, was still weeping. Alec, the gardener, simply shrugged and smoked a cigarette. Julien, their cook, gave Penelope a grim look.

"It is." He cast a glance at Sara, who quieted a bit as she stared back at him.

Penelope noted something unspoken pass between them and thought of the best way to get them to reveal what it was. "I fear they are going to charge Monsieur Martell with murder, though I can't imagine why he would want to kill his wife."

"He would not," Sara insisted, all her sniffles and tears gone under her overriding sense of outrage. "Monsieur loved her very much."

"I'm sure. However, many men who *seem* to love their wives still—"

"*Non!* He would never. He took such great care of her, so sick she was. When they first moved here two months ago, she was already so sick, she did not want to eat or even leave her bedroom. He was the one to make sure she ate, took her medicine, had some time in the sun as the doctor insisted. Monsieur wanted children so badly and she..." She shook her head with dismay, her mouth set with anger.

"Did he know what was wrong with her?"

Sara hiccuped a bitter laugh and shook her head. "I blame that hotel. She never recovered from that horrible woman purchasing it and expelling them. Do you know, she had the audacity to come here." Sara shook her head at the gall of it. "After all she had done, I did not blame Madame for not seeing her, or even the much more pliant daughter who came with her. It was Monsieur who had to take that woman away and make it quite clear she was not to return," Sara said, a note of pride in her voice.

Pen was beginning to suspect Sara had a bit of a crush on *Monsieur*. Perhaps it was simply admiration for how he had cared for his wife.

"When was this?"

"Two or three weeks past?" Sara said after some thought. "It only made Madame more ill. I knew Monsieur's wish for a family would never come true. She would never give him the children he wanted. She even suggested adoption, but Monsieur insisted they should keep—"

"*Sara,*" Julien hissed, censuring her for how much information she was revealing.

"What does it matter now? She is dead and Mademoiselle is correct, they will arrest him for murder!"

Pen thought it rather tactless to be so nakedly honest, but she certainly wasn't going to protest. What had Sara been about to say? It would be just as tactless of her to ask at that point. Pen also wondered what Vera had come to discuss with the Martells. It was no doubt Prynne, her constant companion, who had come with her.

"Madame Martell thought she was being punished for something. Do you know what that might have been? "

Alec snorted and muttered under his breath. Julien looked at him as though offended he had made even that slight contribution to the discussion.

"Do you know something?" Pen asked Alec, despite that.

"Non," Alec grumbled, shaking his head.

"I didn't mean to pry. I was only wondering why Monsieur Martell might have had reason to..." She let the suggestion trail off, hoping any of them would say something.

"He did nothing! I'm sure of it!" Sara insisted.

"Sara," Julien said with a sigh.

Alec grumbled something in French under his breath again that Penelope couldn't quite catch.

Inspector Cloutier returned with Richard. Both of them had no doubt heard at least part of Sara's rant.

"Mademoiselle Banks, I will see you now."

He took her into a small study where they both took armchairs. Before he could begin his interrogation, Penelope decided to ask the question that had been eating at her since his arrival. "Was it in fact Finlay you were here to arrest?"

Inspector Cloutier's lips pressed together with irritation. "I cannot answer that."

"It had to be, as she was the one to give Prynne the drink for her mother. And after all, Finlay had made the threat to Vera earlier in the evening. Unless you think it was George who put the poison in, hoping it would kill his wife? But you'd have no reason to suspect that. At least until today, I suppose. Have you released Marc?"

Inspector Cloutier simply stared at her without comment. Pen sighed and asked no further questions.

"*Alors,*" the inspector said with satisfaction, "please tell me the events leading up to Madame Martell's death, if you please."

"What Richard told you earlier fairly sums up what happened."

"And now I would like it from you...in detail, *s'il vous plaît.*"

She began from the moment Sara opened the door for them.

"Why did she change clothing?" Inspector Cloutier interrupted. "Was she so indecent? Why wait so long to change?"

"I suppose she only realized it at that point. I certainly wouldn't feel very comfortable greeting strangers in a simple shift dress and barefoot."

"Strangers? And yet you came to visit without invitation?"

"I *had* been introduced to Finlay last week, though it wasn't a formal introduction. This had been more of a welfare call. We do plan on staying in Antibes for some months, so it made sense to get to know our fellow Americans."

He didn't bother hiding his skepticism, fully aware by now how meddlesome Penelope could be. Still, he left that without comment.

"You mentioned the garden. Why was she interested in having you view it?"

"I suppose she wanted us to admire the peonies."

"You and Monsieur Prescott both turned? So you would not have seen either of the Martells at that point?"

"I didn't. I doubt Richard did either."

Inspector Cloutier nodded as though Richard had told him as much. "And for how long did you turn to admire the garden?"

"Several seconds." Long enough for the drink to be poisoned without either Pen or Richard seeing it.

Penelope hesitated before divulging the more sensitive portion of the interview. "Finlay did mention that she felt she was being punished for something. She never said what it was."

"Perhaps Madame Tynehook's murder?" He arched a brow in interest.

Pen shook her head. "No, this was in relation to...well, their inability to have children thus far."

His brow lowered. "I see."

"Perhaps the staff will know more."

"*Oui*, please continue."

Penelope continued, telling him about Finlay's request for a splash of gin in her drink, George obliging her, the discussion of Marc's arrest, and then her sudden swooning until she slumped in her chair.

When she was done, Inspector Cloutier stared at his notes, then closed them and studied her for a moment before speaking. "Did Monsieur Martell give any indication that he intended to murder his wife?"

"No, he seemed rather jovial, in fact. If anything, he seemed reluctant to add gin to Finlay's drink. She had to insist."

"Could that have simply been a ruse?"

"I suppose so, but how was he to know she'd even ask?"

"Perhaps he simply took advantage of the opportunity?"

"Perhaps. But why do it with guests in attendance? He could have poisoned her at any time when we weren't there."

Inspector Cloutier shrugged and gave her a questioning look.

"I can't explain it."

"Could Madame Martell have done it herself?"

So that was an avenue the police were considering, after all. "And then suggest her husband put too much gin in? She had to know the finger would be pointed at him."

"Perhaps that was exactly her intent?"

"But why?"

"Because she realized he may have been the one to originally poison her?"

"Do you have reason to believe that?"

"Do you, Mademoiselle Banks?"

"He seemed rather attentive and what would be the motive to poison her at the party?"

"What are the usual motives?"

"Too many to count: anger, greed, jealousy, self-preservation..." Perhaps there *weren't* too many to count. Penelope noted the way Inspector Cloutier looked at her. "What are you thinking?"

He tilted his head to the side and gave her a considering look. "I was simply thinking that you seem to have a very inquisitive mind. As an inspector, I have certain allowances at my disposal. For example, I can find out which of the Martell couple was able to purchase this very fine home."

That would certainly answer a lot, and lend credence to the motive of greed.

"That, in and of itself, may not be enough to firmly settle the case, you see. I could question and interrogate, but I do not have the ear of those closest to the two victims. These Americans are...quite stubborn, I've learned. Quite insistent on their freedoms and rights."

"We learned quite a bit from the French." That earned her a begrudging smile. She considered the inspector through narrowed eyes. "Are you suggesting I use my connections to learn more about the Martells and Mrs. Tynehook? Do a bit of sleuthing on my own?"

"I am doing no such thing." He gave her a meaningful arch of the brow. "But...if you should happen to hear of things, it may be useful."

"I see..."

"The only caution I have—*non*, this is something I must *insist* on, Mademoiselle Banks. You must not reveal anything of the *two* poisons. No one must know there may be two attempts at murder. If it were suspected we had come here to make an arrest for Madame Tynehook's murder, others might feel free to—how do you say it?—let down their guard"

Penelope saw his point. "I understand quite clearly, Inspector Cloutier."

CHAPTER SEVENTEEN

P enelope and Richard left the Martell household, now secured by several policemen. They walked in silence for a while, making their way through Antibes and down to the beach where the rest of their party was.

"What do you suppose it was that killed Finlay?" Penelope asked Richard.

"Some kind of sedative. My guess would be an opiate of some sort."

"So, it was an altogether different poison. It was certainly a more peaceful way to go than Vera's death." Was it George being considerate of the wife he simply wanted gone? Or was it Finlay making her own exit out of life as painless as possible?

"Three poisons in less than twenty-four hours. This certainly is an interesting case."

"You assume they are connected then?"

"Don't you?"

"I do, but the question remains, how? And before you attack me with your usual caution of allowing the police to investigate, Inspector Cloutier all but insisted I do a little digging on my own."

"As he did for me."

"What?" Penelope stopped, forcing Richard to do the same as she turned to him. "He asked you to do your own bit of sleuthing as well?"

"I am a detective after all." He gave her a subtle smile. "Are you upset you weren't the only one? Frankly, I should be the offended party, I think. I'm a professional."

"And I'm not?"

"I don't know how to answer that in a way that won't have me finding a hotel to reside at for the remainder of our stay in Antibes."

"Don't be silly, I'm not a shrew," Penelope said, urging them on again. "I suppose we do work well as a team. And in this case, you can't wag your finger at me."

"Oh, I suspect there will still be plenty of finger-wagging to be had. You are quite meddlesome, my dear."

Penelope stopped yet again. Richard couldn't hold back his laughter at his little jab. After a moment, neither could she.

"Oh, I suppose it's all for the greater good," Pen said, her laughter dying once she remembered the morbid circumstances. "Still, for the sake of our combined sanity, we shouldn't extend the liberty to everyone else. I trust Lulu to be sensible, but Benny and Cousin Cordelia would make a sport of it."

"Agreed."

"Who do you suppose might be inclined to know more?"

Richard cast a glance her way. Penelope sighed and nodded. "Yes, Estelle. She does seem to be up to date on all the scuttlebutt. And I am curious about that Sawyer fellow of hers. What is his story? Why was Vera even interested in him and his Wisconsin connection?"

"Perhaps our professional gossip mongers have been plying their skills in our absence."

In their hurry to know more, they quickly caught a taxi to take them the short distance to the beach. They saw the three others in their party, lying listlessly in the afternoon sun.

"I had no idea lounging on the beach could seem like such strenuous work," Pen said with a smile as she approached.

Benny was the first to greet them with a frown. "We were one moment away from sending the calvary. Poor Cordelia feared they had arrested you as well. What in heaven's name took you so long?"

Penelope and Richard eyed one another. She knew Inspector Cloutier had given him the same suggestion about flushing out the second poisoner by not revealing there had been two poisons. "That's perhaps best left for later. Why don't we go back to the villa for a late lunch? I'm famished."

"Oh yes, please," Cousin Cordelia said with a sense of relief. "I never knew the sun could be this tiring."

They packed up their things and trudged across the beach to leave. They caught a passing taxi to lazily take them back to the villa. It was only once they were in the confines of the home and draped over the living room furniture with cold drinks in their hands that Benny finally sprung on Pen and Richard.

"Alright, tell all, dove. I know you discovered something positively delicious."

Penelope once again looked at Richard. He was the one to speak.

"We stopped by the Commissariat de Police. They

confirmed that Marc had been arrested, but not for murder." He cast a look at Penelope before continuing. She knew he too hated lying to their friends—and there would be hell to pay once the truth came out—but it was a necessary evil. The fewer people who knew the truth, the better. "We decided to visit the Martells while we were out."

"Without us?" Benny shot Pen a sore look.

"There was no need to overwhelm them with all five of us, especially after such a harrowing night," Penelope said. "In fact, it's probably best that you weren't there as...well, I'm afraid Finlay is dead. She's also been poisoned it seems."

The reactions were as expected. Lulu looked surprised, then just as quickly, thoughtful. Benny looked shocked but more so curious about the details. Cousin Cordelia looked as though she might faint. Richard was quick to come to her side.

"Are you alright, Cousin?" Pen gave her a worried look.

"I'm fine dear, just a bit shaken by all this...murder." Cousin Cordelia straightened up from her slump.

"You did ask me not to treat you with kid gloves, so I'm telling you everything." And tell them everything, she did, at least as far as what happened at the Martells.

"It was that husband of hers, I'm certain of it!" Cousin Cordelia stated unequivocally. "I suspected something slimy about him from the onset."

"Oh?" Pen said, giving her a questioning look.

"Yes, I just...well, a woman *knows*." She gave a firm nod to support her accusation.

"What says you, Lulu? You're a woman as well."

"The timing is interesting."

"How do you mean?"

"Why do the deed while you two are there? He had to know the guilt might fall on him. Or perhaps it was Finlay looking for an audience?" Lulu leaned in. "Which scenario makes more sense to you? This husband of hers, taking her glass right in front of two witnesses, filling it with poison, then handing it back to his wife to drink? Or Finlay slipping it in herself, after hand-delivering her husband means and opportunity?"

"That's a good point," Richard said.

"But why kill herself?" Benny said, throwing his hands up.

"Perhaps it was this thing she feels she's being punished for?" Cousin Cordelia hedged, apparently changing her mind about who was guilty.

"The thing her husband was awfully quick to silence her about," Lulu said.

"He probably didn't want her broaching the topic of their troubles starting a family," Cousin Cordelia said.

"Perhaps." Penelope thought it over. "I just feel like there's a connection to it all. This punishment. George quickly silencing her. Finlay making him look guilty."

"Hell hath no fury like a woman scorned," Benny murmured.

"So the real question is, what did George do to incur her scorn?"

They were interrupted by Irma, who handed Penelope an envelope that looked decidedly like an invitation.

"Is it another party?" Benny asked.

"Who would be callous enough to host a party so soon after a murder—*two* murders!" Cousin Cordelia protested.

"Whatever it is, I doubt the sender was aware of Finlay's death when they sent it," Richard said.

"It's from the Tynehooks," Penelope said, which had her quickly opening the envelope. She read the card inside. "It seems we've been invited to a memorial gathering in honor of Vera Tynehook. It's to be held at Chez Monet tonight."

"That sounds decidedly like a bar," Benny said, walking over to look over Pen's shoulders with sudden interest. "Who knew they had a bit of the Irish in them?"

"Do you mean a wake? So soon?" Cousin Cordelia asked. "Their mother has only just passed last night."

"Perhaps it's a chance for them to do their own bit of sleuthing, flush out who poisoned her," Lulu suggested.

"Perhaps this is simply their way of honoring the loss of their mother," Pen said.

"There's no point in speculating," Richard said. "But I don't see the harm in going. We might learn something, especially if there's drinking to be had."

"It would be rude not to go," Cousin Cordelia said, doing a rather fine job of getting over her own disapproval.

Penelope agreed, but not for the same sordid interests. Two young women had lost their mother and wanted company. Or so it would seem. Still, she couldn't help feeling that the sleuthing done that night would be a two-way affair.

CHAPTER EIGHTEEN

Chez Monet was a surprisingly small establishment. It had the standard charming French exterior of a striped awning, small outdoor tables, and painted script on the walls that hinted it served as a cafe during the daylight hours. That late at night, it had indeed been converted into a bar, serving nothing but alcohol. The sounds of lively piano playing reached their ears as they exited their taxi.

"So it would seem this isn't a sad affair then," Benny surmised, not unhappy about that notion.

The door was wide open and, through it, Penelope could see how the place had earned its name. Murals replicating Monet's most famous garden paintings covered the walls. When they entered, Penelope could see there weren't very many people inside, perhaps about fifteen or so. Her eyes assessed it was the group of people she'd hoped would be there: all possible suspects in Vera's murder—save for George and Finlay, of course. Even Julia was in attendance, there to greet them at the door as they entered.

Now, Penelope was even more certain the Tynehook daughters wanted to flush out the person who had poisoned their mother. Or simply assess how many people thought one or both of them were the guilty party.

"Good evening, thank you for coming," Julia said, her expression appropriately somber, despite the snappy tune Peter was tickling along the ivories further inside. It was the first time Penelope had heard her voice, and she was surprised to find she was also American. For some reason, she'd had it in her head that Julia had been hired in France.

"Thank you for inviting us. I didn't know Mrs. Tynehook all that well, but you have my condolences."

Pen studied her reaction. Save for a cynical little quirk at the corners of her mouth, there was nothing to indicate she was pleased about the death.

"I suppose you'll be returning to the United States soon?"

Julia blinked in surprise. "No, of course not. I shall stay here with Miss Tynehook—both of them," she quickly added. Pen wondered which of the Misses Tynehooks she felt was her priority.

Any further prodding would have been awkward at that point so Penelope followed her friends further in.

"You came," Estelle said, instantly rushing over with an exaggerated expression of sorrow on her face. "Isn't it terrible? First Vera, now Finlay?"

"It is," Penelope said, giving her a warning look should she attempt to pry, especially without any pretense of idle chatter beforehand.

"Come, come, let's get you all drinks. We've been raising our glasses in toast all night."

As she was personally dragged toward the bar, Penelope scanned the room again. She spotted Prynne, as still as a statue at a table to herself. She was dressed in black, which did nothing to flatter her. Even in the soft glow of the warm lighting of the bar, she looked pallid and frail. She held a glass of wine that she didn't even seem to be aware of as she stared straight ahead. Those around her cast surreptitious looks of concern and curiosity, no doubt wondering if it was wise to approach her.

Lily leaned against the upright piano at which Peter was playing, though her attention was tightly focused on the newest arrivals. When Pen caught her eye, she didn't bother looking away, instead staring with even more intensity, as though trying to read her for clues.

Peter ignored everyone, his only focus on the keys before him. His hands danced across them with ease. He had a cigarette hanging from the side of his mouth as he crooned. He was quite drunk and the lyrics seemed improvised on the spot:

Those rainy days of April may bring gloom
But May revives us with its dizzy bloom
The seasons come and seasons go
They say you reap that which you sow
But lavender will always be my gal
That purple bloom has cast it's heady spell

Penelope supposed it was meant to be some ode to the cycle of life. Though the note about lavender was interesting. It seemed to be a common theme. They were the flowers Lily held when Pen had first seen her. Were they her favorite? Odd, since it also seemed to be Vera's scent, from what Pen remembered at the party.

Sawyer looked as though he had already finished a full bottle of something strong. He swayed to the music, his face ragged and angry. Pen decided he wouldn't be the first person she approached once she had her drink. However, she was still curious about him.

"Sawyer seems particularly upset," she said to Estelle, who had been leaning over the bar to order them glasses of champagne.

Estelle turned to look over her shoulder at the man who had accompanied her to Antibes. "Yes, he was particularly fond of Finlay." She slid her eyes to Penelope. "Who would have thought George could do such a thing?"

Rather than take that bait, Penelope took one of the glasses of champagne just poured and busied her mouth with it.

"Who, indeed," Benny said, reaching between the two of them to get his glass. He studied Estelle. "So that comes as a surprise to you?"

"Of course," she said innocently. "He seemed so terribly in love."

"You don't suppose he married her for her money?"

"Benny!" Cousin Cordelia scolded, looking scandalized.

Penelope was just glad he'd been the one tactless enough to ask with such frankness.

Estelle's mouth twisted with cynical amusement. "Look at you, rooting in the soil for morsels of gossip."

"Are there any morsels to be had?"

Estelle rolled her eyes. "Yes, Finlay was the one with family money." She saw Pen's look of surprise. "You didn't realize?"

Finlay's statement that her family had been opposed to the marriage now made sense. George's obsession with having children also made sense. What better way to keep a woman from considering divorce? She wondered what would happen to Finlay's money now that she was dead.

Perhaps he had been the one to poison her, after all.

Estelle continued. "But they've been married for almost three years now. Why pick today to rid himself of her?"

"Only three years?" Penelope asked. She'd been certain that Finlay was in her early to mid-thirties. Perhaps whatever was ailing her had made her appear older than she really was.

"Yes, I know. She was already thirty-one when they married. Practically an old maid." Penelope silenced the retort that came to her tongue. Everyone had their reasons for waiting to marry. She wondered what Finlay's had been, especially when Estelle added, "Odd, because apparently, she was quite the catch. Once upon a time, she was a stunning beauty, or so I've been told. And with money? Men should have been lining up. One wonders what the delay was."

"You certainly seem to know a lot about her," Richard said, studying Estelle over his glass.

"Well, one hears things," she idly replied with a flash of a smile. "We are such an incestuous bunch here in Antibes."

"Odd, since America is so large."

"Even New York feels like home when one is in foreign lands, and I've never even stepped foot in that city."

"I wish I could say the same about Santa Barbara. I know nothing about it."

Estelle laughed. "That's hardly comparable. Nothing more than a sleepy little beach town. Beautiful...but dull." She sharpened her gaze. "Speaking of dull, this conversation is the very definition. I suppose I should be the one gauche enough to ask exactly what happened at—"

"Is it true?" Lily stormed their way, leaving a swath of stunned faces in her wake. "Did he kill her?"

The question was directed at Penelope, though it

presented as more of a demand. She was too stunned to answer at first, so Richard did in her place.

"If you're referring to Mr. Martell, the police have taken him into custody," he said, leaving that open to interpretation.

"But you were there. Everyone has said he killed her. Did he?"

"Neither Richard nor I saw anything that could give a definite answer," Penelope said, finding her voice. "I just don't know."

"But the police arrested him. Why would he kill her? Was it because she knew something—something about what happened to mother? Or because...?"

"Because he thought she had been the one to poison her?" Penelope finished for her.

Lily raised her head, staring at Pen as though realizing she was still there. "He shouldn't have done it. He had no business killing her! No reason to! Finlay was so kind and considerate and..." Lily became distraught. "It's all just so... pointless! It makes no sense."

"Do you have reason to believe he didn't kill Finlay?" Estelle prodded.

Lily's head snapped around and she met Estelle with a vicious glare. "You'd love that, wouldn't you? You've had your grubby eyes on George since you got here. It's pathetic really. And Finlay was so blind to it all. I wouldn't be surprised if you had something to do with this."

Estelle looked as if she had been slapped. The sudden quiet in the bar on the heels of it had her face going beet red. Even Peter stopped playing the piano.

Pen decided to interject. "Lily, perhaps—"

"Oh, just—just..." Without finishing, she broke down in tears and ran out of the bar.

"Lily!" Prynne called after her, jerked out of her stupor by the sight of her sister cutting across the room and out the door. She stared after Lily, her eyes wide with alarm.

Peter's hands crashed against the piano keys, lending a discordant tone to the atmosphere, before he jumped up and ran after her. He was stopped at the front door by Julia, of all people.

"Let her go. You're better served here, I think. She should have a moment to herself."

The entire scenario had not only been shocking, but utterly confusing to Penelope. Why did Lily care so much about Finlay's death? What was that accusation toward Estelle about? Why did Julia feel the need to stop Peter fleeing after Lily?

Pen looked around the bar at those still there. Someone in that room had answers, and she saw no reason to avoid trying to discover them.

CHAPTER NINETEEN

"Well...I suppose Lily is just terribly upset," Estelle said, adding a little laugh to help erase her embarrassment at Lily's verbal assault.

Penelope and her friends remained tactfully silent on the matter. She certainly had no information by which to judge Lily's accusation that Estelle was amorously interested in George. However, she was curious about something else Lily had said before fleeing the bar.

"Were Lily and Finlay close?"

"Not that I noticed, though anyone would have sympathized with the poor girl. As you know, Vera was a terror. Lily is obviously still distraught over everything that's happened and taking it out on those around her. Though, now that I think on it, she wasn't so terribly upset after Vera's death, didn't you notice?"

What Penelope noticed was that Estelle was shifting the focus—and guilt—right back on Lily.

Behind them, a crash disrupted any further discussion. Sawyer had drunkenly stumbled into a table, knocking it over. The couple who had been seated there, jumped away, voicing their protests.

"*Sawyer*," Estelle muttered in exasperation.

"Allow me to handle this," Richard said, walking over to grab him and escort him into a corner, away from other potential paths of destruction.

"I think perhaps I should offer my condolences to poor Miss Tynehook," Benny said, looking far too sympathetic for Pen to believe it was completely genuine.

"I'll go with you," Cousin Cordelia said, giving him a skeptical look. "The poor girl has just lost her mother, after all."

Pen shot her a grateful smile while Benny rolled his eyes.

"I suppose that leaves me to the ivory tickler," Lulu said, giving Pen a droll look. "Perhaps I can get that man to play something more fitting for the occasion than this business about Mother Nature."

"Such an efficient team you have there," Estelle said, watching the last of Pen's friends leave. "One might just accuse you all of strategy."

"Aren't we all curious as to who killed Mrs. Tynehook?" Pen said, arching an eyebrow. "Since we're on the topic, you had just as much means and opportunity as Lily did."

"*Moi*?" Estelle pressed a hand to her chest and gave Pen an exaggerated look of indignation.

"What is it you whispered to Prynne while Peter was playing last night?"

Estelle smiled conspiratorially. "Something she should have already known, but was too...*preoccupied* to notice."

A perfect non-answer. Pen knew pressing the issue wouldn't get her an honest response. Why was Estelle suddenly so shy about divulging information?

"Lily *is* right though, I was interested in George. Who wouldn't be? He was handsome and charming. But he was depressingly devoted to Finlay. He'd wake up bright and early each morning just to buy her flowers. A true romantic, or so I thought."

Pen was surprised at the confession. "He was also wealthy. Or would be once Finlay was gone."

Estelle laughed, loudly enough to incur a few curious looks. "True. And I won't lie, that made it easy to keep my hands off."

"I'm sure."

"So you now think he killed Finlay?"

Penelope didn't answer. Truthfully, she still couldn't see it. He'd have to have known the finger would be pointed at him, and him alone.

"By golly...you don't!" Estelle stood up straighter at the realization. She stared at Pen with wide eyes. "So you think...Finlay killed herself? But why?"

"I haven't said anything, one way or the other," Pen replied in an irritated voice. She certainly didn't want that rumor spread, not without bona fide proof.

"You don't have to, sweetheart. I'm good at reading people." Estelle smirked. "I suppose the question is, why?"

"You seem to know everything that goes on. Why do you suppose she might have killed herself?"

"She was awfully sick. Neither of them ever gave a definite answer as to what was wrong with her. My money was on cancer; horrid way to go. Perhaps she took a quicker way out?"

"In front of guests?" And all while suggesting her husband may have done it? Pen wisely kept that part to herself.

"Hmm, that is a puzzle."

Once again, the conversation was interrupted by another bit of chaos from Sawyer. Richard's temporary hold on him had reached its limits.

"Get off me, you fool!" Sawyer pushed Richard away and teetered on two feet, stumbling from the corner. He grabbed a glass of something from a random table and drank from it. "I loved her, and that...*bastard*, he killed her!"

Well now....

Penelope was intrigued, but not entirely surprised, in retrospect. That little interaction between George and Sawyer at Vera's party had hinted at something like this. Pen chanced a glance at Estelle, only to find her looking on with bored indifference. So her connection to Sawyer truly was a platonic relationship of convenience.

Penelope watched Sawyer finish off the drink in his hand, then throw it to the ground in a crash. Despite his drunken state, he managed to stay upright enough to stumble out of the bar, fading into the darkness beyond the entrance.

"The Wisconsin connection," Penelope muttered, suddenly putting it in place.

"What's that?" Estelle asked.

Penelope ignored her, quickly leaving the bar to follow Sawyer out and confirm her suspicions.

CHAPTER TWENTY

I t was only when Penelope was outside that she had misgivings about following Sawyer out of the bar. She shook it off. He was drunk, not dangerous. Yes, angry, but mostly out of grief it seemed. At worst, he would be verbally abusive, but he had no reason to harm her. Even once she revealed the secret she suspected he held.

That spurred Pen on, rushing in the direction she'd seen him headed. She saw his figure further ahead, still teetering as he ambled down the sidewalk, occasionally stumbling into the street. The few people out that late at night under-standably made a wide berth around him. The street lights and the glow from other bars cast a light around him as he passed, like a flashing beacon. And with each pass, Pen saw what she had seen just before he'd disappeared from view at Chez Monet.

The reddish color of his blonde hair.

That first day on the beach, his hair had either held a golden hue in direct sunlight or darkened into something dirtier in the shade. At Vera's party the night before, there had been so much lighting, bouncing off the stark white walls, that his hair had seemed at most a sort of strawberry blonde. It hadn't been enough for Penelope to connect him to the words written in Vera's diary. Now, she had reason to wonder.

"Sawyer!"

He stopped and stood there, as though unsure if he had actually heard his name. She called out again, and he awkwardly turned in place, frowning at Pen as she approached him.

He was in half-shadow underneath the furthest reach of the nearest light, and she studied him. Yes, his hair was reddish enough to just barely be included in the category of a redhead. But there was something about him, particularly in connection to Finlay, that still didn't seem to fit. They had barely acknowledged one another the few times Pen had seen them together.

"I'm terribly sorry about Finlay."

"Did he do it?"

"I..." Penelope had gone back and forth so many times now, she wasn't sure. "I honestly don't know."

His eyes narrowed. "He did. She should have never married him."

"You knew her because she's from Wisconsin too?"

He gave her a puzzled look. "How'd you know that?"

"So it's true." She mulled that over, still studying him.

"I've always loved her," he lamented.

Suddenly she realized what it was that bothered her. "No...it wasn't you. Estelle said you were the youngest. It was an older brother. He was the one Finlay was involved with. I suspect his hair is much redder than yours?"

Again his brow wrinkled in puzzlement, wondering

how she knew. "Patrick? Yes, redder than mine. But not nearly as much as Kenneth or Walt."

So, that was the red hair connection. The reference to Santa Barbara was simply to flush out who Estelle really was. Perhaps specifically because she had arrived in Antibes with Sawyer.

Why was Vera so interested in Sawyer? Or perhaps it was Finlay she was focused on?

"Tell me about her."

A bitter twist came to Sawyer's mouth and he looked away. "Patty brought her home to Madison after that first year at Marquette. That summer, she stayed with an aunt who lived there, but she was at our place nearly every day. She was seventeen and I was just a dumb kid, only twelve. She treated me like a kid brother, which I should have expected. Still, when you grow up the youngest of four boys, just about anything in a dress is a breath of fresh air. And Finlay was..." Sawyer exhaled and shook his head, then hiccuped a laugh. "Sawyer and Finn—you know, like the Mark Twain books? I only ever called us that in my head, but it felt like it was meant to be. I thought one day she'd realize what an idiot my older brother was and see me as.... Well, anyway, it was a fool's hope. She was dizzy for Patrick."

"What happened between your brother and her?"

He scowled. "Patrick, the idiot, got involved with another girl. I guess one summer was too long for him to actually remain faithful to Finlay. She went home early, without so much as a goodbye. I tried writing to her, fool that I was, but each letter was always returned, unopened. I can't blame her for that. When I went to Marquette University, it was all for Finlay. I tried reconnecting or at least learning something about how things had turned out for her. I was surprised to learn that she hadn't yet married. Of course, that got me thinking dumb things I shouldn't have. I don't even know what I expected to come of it. She was five years older than me, after all. Even beyond that, that family of hers wasn't having it."

Penelope couldn't help but sympathetically smile at how sentimental young love was, even in men. "She's the reason you came to Antibes? Even after all this time?"

He fell against the wall, if only to steady himself while on wobbly feet. "It isn't as though I haven't had my dalliances, even a few gals that everyone thought might lead somewhere. I thought if I could just see her one last time, reassure myself she was happily married and wanted nothing to do with me...or my family. Then maybe I could move on with my life. So, I talked my parents into a summer trip to France, before finally getting serious about someone."

Penelope waited, wondering how that first meeting here in Antibes had gone. She was surprised to see a small smile touch his lips.

"I thought she would once again want nothing to do with me. I would have left Antibes quick as a whip, got drunk every night in Paris until my return home. That's why I partnered with Estelle before we arrived. I thought..." He looked bashful and Pen didn't need to work too hard to figure it out; he'd hoped Estelle might make Finlay jealous. Pen admired Estell for not revealing his true motives.

His expression changed in an instant as he continued. "I expected to find Finlay at least something like she'd been that summer when Patrick brought her home. How could she not be, all this sun and easy living? But she looked terrible, thinner and paler. It was that damn hotel. She had gotten it in her mind to buy it, you see. Fix up what needed fixing and then continue living there along with other Americans, and the Brits when they came down. She was putting her own money into it, begging her family for a little here, a little there, all from the trust they still maintained for her. It wasn't as though George was contributing anything," he spat.

"Were she and George having any problems?"

"They hadn't approved of her marrying George, her family. That's what she told me. We'd become...acquaintances by then. She wouldn't talk about Patrick, and I had no problem with that. I wasn't over her, but I also respected her marriage. I stayed here in Antibes out of concern for her, not just her health. I'm sure that's what led to whatever is ailing her; having to go to her family, hat in hand, every time she needed to fix the roof or repair a wall, or whatnot. Then, her father died two months ago and she inherited her money without strings. Of course by then, Vera had already come in and bought the hotel right from underneath—"

"Two months ago?" Penelope interrupted. "How much did she inherit?"

"I don't know, but the Schroeders certainly weren't lacking in lettuce, if you get my drift. In fact, I'd say they were wealthier than my family. Patty really muddled that drink." He exhaled an ironic laugh, probably noting how muddled he was right now due to drink. All hints of humor left his face. "He did her rotten, and for that, even hell is too good for him. The same goes for George."

Penelope decided to move on, while she still had him. "Can you think of why Finlay might have felt she was being punished for something? Do you know of any scandals in her past?"

Sawyer's gaze darkened for a moment, then he lifted his

chin and looked down his nose at her with offense. "If I did, I fail to see how that would be your business."

He did know something.

"I don't mean to pry, it's just that, while Richard and I were visiting with her today, she stated she felt she was being punished. I can't help but wonder if she may have felt guilty enough to...perhaps take her own life?"

"No!" He viciously shook his head. "She wouldn't have. Not after all this time. Not when she was finally free from her family."

"What about in her past? Something that's come back to haunt her?"

His gaze faltered, a hint of uncertainty touching it. His mouth curled with animosity. "If she did kill herself, it was George that pushed her to it. She was fragile, he would have known that before he even married her. Either way, he was the one who killed her today. I'd swear my life on it."

It was understandable Sawyer would point the finger at the man who had managed to marry the woman for whom he held a candle. Penelope couldn't deny her own suspicions, especially with this new information about Finlay coming into her fortune. But why wait two months to murder her—if it *was* George who had put the poison in her drink?

"Penelope!"

They both turned at the sound of Richard's voice calling out to her. He jogged to quickly reach them, a look of worry on his face.

"Are you alright?"

"I'm fine," Pen said, trying not to sound too dismissive of his concern. Sawyer hadn't exactly been in fine condition when she'd rashly chased after him. "I was just asking Sawyer a few questions."

"Prying, is what," Sawyer spat.

"Yes, prying, and I've learned some interesting developments."

"Speaking of interesting developments, Inspector Cloutier came to the bar not too long after you left. You need to come back with me."

CHAPTER TWENTY-ONE

Penelope urged Sawyer to come back to the bar with them. At least there, any damage he did in his drunken state would be limited. Who knew what he'd be involved in on his own that late at night?

Sawyer had told her exactly what she could do with that idea. Penelope took the vile comments with perfect aplomb, realizing how ossified he was. She'd had to pull Richard away before he followed up with a rather unpleasant response of his own, the kind that may have left Sawyer in worse condition than he already was.

"Does Inspector Cloutier need something from me?"

"We've been called in for an interview."

"At this hour?"

"It seems George Martell has requested an audience with the two of us. He deemed it rather urgent."

"He has? Whatever for?"

"I suppose that is what we're to find out." He slid his eyes to Pen, piercing her with his gaze. "Hopefully Sawyer had something more helpful to offer than his insulting parting words?"

"He did, and you don't have to protect me, Richard. He's hardly the worst man I've ever had to interact with. Or have you forgotten my sordid past frequenting gambling rooms, speakeasies, and other establishments of ill repute?"

"Should I answer as your fiancé or as Detective Prescott?" At least he was finally in a humorous mood.

"Sometimes I wonder if there is a difference," Pen said with a smirk. "But put your detective hat on for this bit of news. Sawyer has known Finlay since he was twelve. His older *red-haired* brother had a romantic summer with her; left her brokenhearted. There's your Wisconsin connection."

"Ah, let me guess, Mr. Hendricks admired her from afar back then."

"First loves do tend to leave an imprint on the heart, particularly when they are unrequited."

"There are also more dangerous reactions to unrequited love."

"If I can't have her, no one can? I doubt that's the case with Sawyer, not after so long. He seemed more concerned about her health than anything. Of course, he was adamant that George had done the poisoning."

"Of course."

"There's something odd going on here. Finlay. George. Sawyer. Even Estelle. I don't understand why Vera had an interest in all of them."

"Perhaps George will provide some insight."

The bar was quieter now, everyone staring at Inspector Cloutier with cautious, curious eyes. Peter had stepped away from the piano and was having a conversation with Prynne. She seemed to be asking something of him, and he didn't seem happy about it, more irritated than anything.

The inspector approached Penelope and Richard, an

apologetic look on his face. "I am sorry for the hour. However, when I learned of this, ah, gathering, I thought perhaps I might be impertinent with my request. Monsieur Martell was quite adamant in his wishes to speak to you."

Just the mention of his name had a few backs stiffening in response, people leaning in with more interest. Pen saw her friends gathered near the bar. She wondered what they had learned, if anything, during the evening.

"For the sake of justice, of course we'll go," Penelope said.

Inspector Cloutier nodded, a relieved look on his face as he led the way out of the bar. When they arrived at the Commissariat de Police, they were greeted by M. Travere, who also seemed pleased they had agreed to come. He led them to an interview room but paused before letting them in.

"Inspector Cloutier and I will be in the room as well. That is to remind Monsieur Martell that anything he says may rightfully be included in our investigation, and perhaps used against him during his trial."

"Is his attorney here as well?" Richard asked.

"He declined one."

Richard and Penelope looked at each other in surprise. It was incredibly reckless of him to speak in the presence of the police without his attorney.

When Inspector Cloutier opened the door, they found George sitting on one side of a table. He perked up when the door opened. When Richard and Penelope entered, he exhaled and gave a slight nod, as though things were going according to plan. He gestured to the two chairs across from him, like a host greeting his guests.

Penelope still couldn't fathom why he'd want the two of them there, especially without a lawyer to caution him. She and Richard sat, while the judge and inspector stood behind them, directly in his line of sight.

"Thank you for coming."

"I'm not sure how we can help you," Richard said with a questioning look on his face. Even with his years on the police force, this was probably as unusual for him as it was for Penelope.

"I just want you to listen, tell me if I'm wrong at any point." He glanced past them at the two men standing. "I've tried to tell them how ridiculous all of this is."

"We aren't the jury, Mr. Martell, or the judge, for that matter. Speaking with us doesn't really—"

"I didn't kill my wife!" George insisted, interrupting Richard. He took a moment to collect his thoughts before continuing in a normal tone. "Just, let me walk you through what happened. If anything I say is different from what you remember, feel free to say so."

Penelope and Richard glanced at each other, then back to George, and nodded.

"I hadn't been expecting a visit and was surprised to see you at the door when Sara opened it." He waited for confirmation, and after a moment, Richard and Pen both nodded in agreement. George exhaled and continued. "You were there to see Finlay and I took you back to the sunroom where she'd been most of the day—Sara will confirm that part." His eyes flitted to the two men behind them. "She already had a glass of lemonade. She even took a sip when we first entered the sunroom."

George continued narrating the events of that afternoon. With some adjustment as to periods of time—specifically how long both he and Finlay had disappeared—Richard and Penelope agreed with him.

When he was done, he leaned over the table to pierce

them with his eyes. Richard instinctively sat up straighter, ready to intervene should he get physical.

"I know you're a detective, Mr. Prescott. Estelle told Finlay and me as soon as she could." He grimaced slightly, as though mentioning her name caused him nothing but irritation. "She'll confirm as much, I'm sure. I also know that you, Miss Banks, are a private investigator. Why would I poison my own wife with either of you right there? You saw me take her glass and leave the room, then come back and hand it to her. Am I a fool? Do I seem so incredibly stupid?" He was pleading now.

"Do you have another explanation for her death?" Penelope asked.

"They tell me it was an overdose of laudanum in her glass," George said. "I didn't even know she had laudanum!"

"And yet, we found the bottle in her room, in plain view on her nightstand. It was empty." Inspector Cloutier said. He gave George a grave look. "And also conveniently wiped clean of fingerprints."

George paused, taking a breath to calm himself before he continued. "That has to be it. I don't know how, but she was the one to dose her lemonade, don't you see? Finlay was the one to kill herself. She wiped the prints so no one would know it was her doing and hers alone."

Behind her, Penelope heard Inspector Cloutier snort with disbelief.

"Are you still maintaining that you didn't know about the laudanum?" Penelope asked.

She could see a brief flicker in his eyes, as though he was thinking about lying before he sagged and sighed. "I suspected she had secretly been taking some. She certainly wasn't getting it from Dr. Archambault, the doctor I obtained for her. I suppose she thought it was the only thing that soothed the constant pain she was in, helped her get to sleep. But as the inspector said, the bottle was in *her* room."

"How would she have gotten it into her glass?" Richard pointed out. "She never took her drink with her out of the room. You were the only one to do that. You could have easily gone up to her room during that time."

George exhaled in frustration and put his head in his hands. "I don't know how she did it. Maybe it was in there before you even arrived? Perhaps there was a second bottle? She could have put it there before we joined her."

"We found no such second bottle," Inspector Cloutier insisted.

"Besides, she'd been sipping from her glass the entire time," Penelope pointed out. "With enough in it to kill her, we would have noticed at least some effects before you took her glass away."

"I just don't know!" He sighed and shook his head with frustration. "I loved Finlay but she was troubled, she always has been. Her family, they could—well, I don't suppose they'll offer any testimony on my behalf. But the fact is, she was sick and this isn't the first time she's...well, done something drastic."

Penelope sat up straighter, enough to draw both George's and Richard's attention. "She's done it before, hasn't she? Or at least attempted to. Back in Wisconsin, when she was younger? Perhaps only seventeen?"

George blinked in surprise that she knew so much. "Her family sent her away. A health retreat, they called it. Everyone knows what that really means, especially when you have money. It was really a sanitarium. Her father thought it might scare me away, claimed she was never the same after that. I didn't care, I loved her."

"When did she start getting sick?" Pen asked, curious.

He paused, his mind jumping to more recent history. "Earlier this year."

"So not long after you made the hotel your home?"

"I suppose so," he said in thought. "She loved it so much, she wanted to stay there. I thought it was crazy, she even made noise about buying and running it ourselves. There was a period when she was full of life, and I thought maybe it wasn't such a bad idea. The owners let us do a bit of decorating to our tastes. Finlay had an eye, and wanted to do all of it herself. Perhaps it was the stress of overworking to get it done. Maybe it was the pressure to have children. We'd decided to start trying by then. I don't know, but that's when everything reversed. She became more and more sick."

"This was before Mrs. Tynehook arrived in Antibes?"

He nodded.

So Finlay had been sick before moving to the current Martell residence, despite what Pen had been told.

"Do you know why Mrs. Tynehook bought it?"

"I assume it was strictly for business reasons. Antibes is popular with Americans, and thanks to Finlay and me, the hotel was as well."

"So she had no particular interest in either you or Finlay?"

"Not as far as I know."

"But she did come to visit you at your new home well after the fact? What was that about?"

Again he looked surprised, his eyelids blinking rapidly. He didn't bother asking how she knew this, nor denying it had happened. "She came to make an offer. She wanted us back in the hotel. She understood kicking us out had been unwise. Finlay and I, especially before she became sick, were quite popular here. Vera thought it might encourage more wealthy Americans to stay there. I told her in no uncertain terms we would never go back so long as she owned it. Besides, we had already bought our current house by then. She wasn't happy about that."

"So you didn't consult with Finlay in making that decision?" Pen couldn't help feeling a bit irked by that.

George glared at her. "I'm her husband, I didn't need to consult with her. Besides, anyone would have known she felt the same. You saw how she was at the party. She despised Vera."

"Such unfortunate timing that she managed to buy the hotel just before Finlay came into her inheritance after her father died two months ago."

George's eyes went wide. Penelope had been hoping to surprise him, just to see how he'd react to her bit of knowledge.

"How did you—?" George went quiet and swallowed hard. "I know what you're accusing me of. Yes, it looks bad, but..." He slammed his fist on the table in frustration. "It wasn't me!"

"Calm down, Mr. Martell," Richard warned.

"Who inherits this money now that your wife is dead?" Penelope asked.

George was silent, quietly stewing in a brew he was quickly drowning in.

"We have obtained a copy of Madame Martell's most recent will, dated only a week ago," M. Travere said.

George's eyes flashed with surprise at the announcement. "So soon?"

"We operate quite rapidly when a murder is at hand. Would you like to know what it says? Or perhaps you already know?"

George went back to silently simmering, not bothering to answer.

"Everything is to be divided among her children, either those naturally born or by adoption. But alas, you and Madame Martell have no children, and thus it reverts to you, Monsieur, as stipulated in her will."

The silence on the heels of that was heavy with accusation. Penelope wondered just how eager George was to have children with her, despite his public professions. Sara had mentioned Finlay wanted to try adoption. Pen understood why he might object to that. Finlay's money was now all his.

"Is there anything you can think of, something that might save your case?" Pen asked. She still couldn't fathom why he'd so brazenly poison Finlay in front of them.

He gave her an ironic smile. "No, and I suppose that's exactly how Finlay wanted it."

"Are you now suggesting that your wife has framed you?" Inspector Cloutier sounded incredulous.

"I'm not suggesting it, I'm stating it quite plainly." Now, all that was left in his eyes was defeat. There was nothing more to say.

CHAPTER TWENTY-TWO

B y the time Richard and Penelope made it back to Chez Monet, almost everyone noteworthy had gone home. Benny, Lulu, and Cousin Cordelia sat at a table, all three nursing glasses of wine from the bottle that sat in the middle.

"Huzzah, they return from faraway lands!" Benny announced, quite plainly ossified up to his ears. "Odysseus made his way back to Ithaca in a shorter amount of time."

"It sure felt that long," Lulu said with a weary sigh.

"Heavens, what could that man possibly want that would take so long? We were beginning to worry, yet again, that they had arrested you," Cousin Cordelia said.

"Don't be silly, it wasn't that long, and it wasn't particularly fruitful."

"All that time and not a morsel for us to nibble on?" Benny said with a pout.

"Mr. Martell only succeeded in digging his own hole, I'm afraid," Richard said.

"The better question is, did you all gather any morsels tonight? We still have no idea who killed Vera."

"But let's go home first," Richard suggested. "It's been a weary night."

They managed to find a car to take them home. All five piled into it like lazy sloths, the events of the night and too much drinking catching up with them. As usual, arriving at the villa created a second wind that had them settling into the living room to discuss what they had learned.

Pen was most eager to discover what Benny and Cousin Cordelia had picked up while offering their condolences to Prynne. "Did she give any clues as to who might have killed her mother?"

"We didn't pry, Penelope," Cousin Cordelia protested. "Mostly, we discussed her health. It seems the Antibes air has been doing wonders for her constitution. Though not at first. She was awfully sick when they first arrived, violently so. They all were, though she suffered the worst of it, poor dear. One must acclimate one's self to new environs. My friend Mrs. Tarleton was sick for nearly two weeks when she first moved to New York."

Benny sighed with disappointment. "Yes, yes, but now Prynne is much better, *thriving* even. Such that she feels rather guilty about how robust her constitution is in the wake of her mother's death. Blah, blah, blah, is there any more tedious conversation than one's health, especially in such great detail?" Benny shot Cousin Cordelia a baleful look.

Penelope's cousin pursed her lips. "I only wanted to know if there was something in particular we should be concerned about. One never knows what sort of exotic diseases are in the air in these foreign countries."

"There are so many Americans here, it might as well be the Hamptons," Benny said.

"Fine, but when *you* start breaking out in sores and feeling lethargic, don't say I didn't warn you. I plan on taking myself to the nearest doctor as a precaution, though I shudder to think what strange methods the French use." Cousin Cordelia visibly shuddered.

"Did you say sores?" Penelope asked in alarm.

"Yes, in the beginning. It was terribly frightful for the poor dear. Her mother suffered the same. Lily, fortunately, was immune to it. It was trying enough that Mrs. Tynehook almost changed her mind about purchasing the hotel. Oh! Do you suppose it was that curse at work? To think, they've been living with it since they first came to Antibes!"

"Perhaps the human sacrifice has been enough to release it, dove."

"Don't you joke about curses, Benny," Lulu scolded, slapping him on the arm. "You'll bring that dang curse upon this house."

"I agree, curses are no laughing matter," Cousin Cordelia said. "Even if they have been lifted."

"I don't suppose you discovered anything about curses while lingering near the piano, Lulu?" Penelope asked.

"Only the one that has a hold of that man's heart."

"You mean Lily?" Perhaps Julia had reason to be concerned.

"Lily?" Lulu laughed. "Honey no, that man is positively dizzy for Mademoiselle Prynne."

"Prynne? Are you certain?"

Lulu laughed again and shook her head. "I forget what blinders you have when it comes to secret love affairs."

Penelope scoffed, never mind that she'd certainly had blinders on when it came to Lulu and Tommy Callahan back in New York.

"How can you be certain? He and Lily were awfully flirtatious with one another."

"What I saw was a little girl intent on gettin' her Mama's britches in a hitch by flirting with every inappropriate man she could find. All the better if her mama didn't know who the *real* target of his affection was. No, that Mr. Compton only has eyes for one Tynehook sister."

"Smart choice if he's after money."

"Don't be so cynical, Benny. I find it rather charming, this secret love affair of theirs. Though, is that love requited?" Cousin Cordelia asked, a hopeful look on her face.

Penelope thought back to every interaction between Peter and Prynne. It seemed his coming to Prynne's aid when she fainted had been for her sake, not Lily's. Perhaps Julia didn't disapprove after all and wanted to keep him in the bar with Prynne. In retrospect, he'd only gone after Lily when she stormed off after Prynne had cried out for her. Even that song of his from the party could have been meant for Prynne, as ambiguous as it was. She'd certainly blushed enough during it. Had that been what Estelle had been whispering to Prynne to make her blush that way?

"If Prynne did feel the same about Peter, then that sadly creates even more of a motive to rid herself of an interfering mother," Penelope finally said. The expressions on the faces of everyone in the room indicated they had been thinking the same thing.

"It will be impossible to prove, and that's if she was the one to poison her mother's drink. There are simply too many other suspects who are just as likely to have done it," Richard said. "At least in the case of Finlay's death, we only have two suspects, and even that is proving impossible to solve."

"It may not be," Penelope said, rethinking that day's events. "I suspect there is at least one person in that household who knows more than they've let on. I think a revisit to the Martell home is in order."

CHAPTER TWENTY-THREE

The next morning, Penelope went alone to the Martell home to talk with the staff. Even Richard had agreed it would be easier to get information as a woman on her own than with a detective in tow. Benny had held back his pouting, as a day at the beach was far preferable to prying information from household staff.

It was late enough that Sara would likely be up, despite the lack of anyone to attend to. Penelope assumed they had been paid through the month and, as live-in staff, they would remain at the home until they could find other situations.

Sure enough, Sara was there to open the door when Pen came knocking. She gave Penelope a look of confusion before remembering herself and replacing it with polite solemnity.

"I'm afraid there is no one home at present, mademoiselle." She didn't bother hiding the pointed look on her face.

"I actually came to speak with you, and perhaps Alec and Julien, if they are available."

A guarded expression fell like a mask across Sara's face.

"It may help prove Monsieur Martell's innocence." That hit the exact target Penelope had hoped for and Sara's face softened. She opened the door wider for Pen to enter.

"Alec comes only once a week, but Julien is here. Please, have a seat in the parlor, and I will have him—"

"Actually, I'd like to speak with you first, alone."

Sara paused, once again giving Penelope a cautious look, but she didn't demur.

"The police have determined it was laudanum that caused Madame Martell's death. As the housemaid, you would have seen it, perhaps in her boudoir or personal effects?"

Sara didn't hesitate before answering. "Madame took many things to ease her ailments. But yes, that was among the things in her bedroom."

"Did you see Monsieur Martell go upstairs at all during our visit?"

Sara's face became a shade pinker. "I was busy in the binding room."

"The binding room?"

"*Oui*. Monsieur enjoys binding books for Madame—or, he did." She paused, her face wrinkling with sorrow. "It was a hobby of his. He told me that is how they met. Madame loved books, and he worked at a rare bookshop, rebinding old books."

Penelope recalled the bookcase in the sunroom and the book on the table next to Finlay. They *had* been beautifully bound.

"Monsieur has told me not to bother with that room, as it is his private space. I was simply returning a tool he had left in the hall upon your arrival. It's so rare that I see the room, I confess I was fascinated and remained much longer than I should have to see his work. He would be upset if he knew I'd been in there."

So she wouldn't have seen if George rushed upstairs with Finlay's glass of lemonade.

"I assume you didn't see any bottles of laudanum there?" Pen asked in a dry tone.

Sara shook her head no. "There were a lot of jars and containers, but I cannot tell you what they were."

"I imagine." Pen thought about everything that might be involved in leather-binding books. If George had wanted to poison his wife, there were probably at least a handful of lethal substances at his disposal. At least with laudanum, Finlay didn't suffer. Which was a fine way to go if someone was choosing their own means of death.

"Wait...did you say 'her' bedroom?" Penelope asked, replaying the conversation in her head. Finlay had stated something about having a personal bedroom as well. "So Monsieur and Madame Martell didn't share a bedroom?"

Sara sniffed, as though the question was impertinent.

Penelope ignored her reproach, as understandable as it was. "Can I see her room? I assume the police have already done a search of it."

"*Oui*, they did, and left a horrible mess. The *fille* who cleans only comes twice a week."

Penelope realized she was worried about being judged for her lack of housekeeping. "I certainly don't fault you for not wanting to interfere with a crime scene, especially so soon after Madame Martell's passing."

Sara relaxed, then, after a moment she nodded and led the way up the stairs. Penelope followed her to one end of the hall where she opened the door.

Finlay's room was done in the same green paint as the sunroom, though it didn't have any of the wallpaper yet. It had a decidedly feminine touch, with silk flowers and plants placed around the room and a frilly white bedspread. There was another small case of leather-bound books near a window and a small armchair for her to sit and read in. If it weren't for the beauty of Antibes outside, Penelope could understand why it would be difficult to leave such a lovely room.

"When did Monsieur Martell move into his own bedroom?"

Sara exhaled a noise of indignation.

"Please, Sara. It could be important." It wasn't as though it was uncommon for a husband and wife to have separate bedrooms, especially if they could afford it. Her own parents had.

"They have always maintained separate rooms. Madame suffered so, especially at night. She thought it best for him to have a more peaceful sleep, so he took the next room. It is much smaller. He wanted her to be more comfortable," she said with a note of admiration in her voice.

"May I see his room?"

Again she gave her a look of indignation. Penelope sighed internally before once again uttering the magic words. "It could help prove his innocence."

Sara's expression became dubious, but she nodded and led her out of Finlay's bedroom to the next room down the hall. She opened it and gave Penelope a piercing look before allowing her to pass through.

George's room was much smaller and noticeably more stark. The walls were still white and there was little in the way of decoration. The only furniture was an armoire, desk, and bed, though all were made of good quality and construction. Unlike the chintzy curtains in the much larger bedroom, George had simple bare, Venetian blinds. He certainly wasn't living like a monk, as the bed looked more than comfortable and the desk was quite ornate, but he had sacrificed to give Finlay the larger room.

Penelope wandered to the desk, hoping to see something relevant. In view, there were mostly invoices and receipts. As she ambled closer to get a better look, Sara cleared her throat.

"I think that is all for now."

Pen spun around and smiled. "Of course. I certainly didn't mean to snoop."

Sara pursed her lips and gestured back toward the hallway. Penelope led the way out and down the stairs, feeling rather pleased. She had gotten enough of a look to have everything on that desk perfectly recorded in her head. Something to refer to later on.

"You said Alec only came in once a week. Do you have an address for him? Perhaps a phone number?"

Sara studied her, a wrinkle of doubt in her brow. "Alec does not have a phone, but I will give you his address."

After obtaining the address, Penelope had a brief conversation with Julien, mostly regarding Finlay's rather bland diet, on doctor's orders. It was no wonder she looked so pale and thin. But he had nothing more relevant to offer.

Penelope thanked them both, then left. She was interested to see what Alec had to say. The day before when he had snorted in response to her inquiry about Finlay had her particularly curious.

She made her way closer to the center of town where she could hire a taxi, assuming the driver would be familiar with the address Sara had given her. The one she caught, gave her an uncertain look, eyeing her expensive clothes.

"Are you certain, mademoiselle?"

"*Oui*, I am."

He shrugged and drove them through the streets of Antibes, further away from the villas and pretty shops for tourists. The buildings were closer together and less well-maintained in this part of town. The taxi wound through narrow alleyways before coming to a stop at one with an unassuming door that was badly in need of a fresh coat of paint.

"Will you wait here? I'll pay for the full time...plus extra for your consideration." By way of example, Pen paid the fare to get there plus a few additional francs.

The taxi driver shrugged and grunted something that was close enough to a yes. Penelope got out and walked to the front door. By now it was late morning, so she hoped she wasn't waking Alec. He already seemed like a cantankerous sort, and she didn't want him too grumpy to answer a few questions.

After knocking on the door, Pen waited. At first, she was certain he might not be home. After a second knock to be sure, she heard an angry slew of French words on the other side.

It took a full minute for Alec to answer, and he didn't look pleased. But he was surprised to see Penelope standing there. He stared in confusion before demanding to know what she wanted. "Qu'est-ce que tu veux?"

Penelope responded to him in French. "*I apologize for intruding on you, but I wanted to ask a question about Madame Martell.*"

A sly look came to his face and one side of his mouth hitched up with amusement. "*Why should I speak to you?*"

"*Don't you care about who may have murdered her?*"

He grunted his lack of concern with regard to that matter.

She pulled out a franc note. *"And do you care about this?"*

That earned her a snort of approval and he snatched the bill, then opened the door wider for her. Pen hesitated before entering. He wasn't the most friendly character but at the very least he lacked the motivation to harm her.

The inside was surprisingly tidy, though reflected the impoverishment of the neighborhood outside. He didn't offer her anything but a seat, and Pen was happy to oblige. He took a comfortable but well-worn armchair for himself.

She continued speaking in French. *"Yesterday you seemed to know why Madame Martell may have felt she was being punished. What was it?"*

He grinned, savoring it for a bit before answering. *"Madame was not as sick as she claimed, at least not too sick to..."* He finished with a word Penelope wasn't familiar with, but she caught the gist of it.

"Are you saying Madame Martell was having an affair?"

He shrugged noncommittally. *"I only say what I saw. She would go out on her own while Monsieur was out. I saw who she met with."*

"She met with someone? A man?"

A sly smile spread his lips and he nodded. *"At a secluded cafe...not the kind you Americans bother with."*

"Again, do you think she was having an affair?"

He shrugged but the suggestive look on his face answered the question.

"You said it wasn't a cafe Americans would go to. Was he French?"

His mouth turned down and he looked skeptical. *"I do not think so. It was the hat, the way he wore it, a silly thing with a striped band. He was American."*

That wasn't much to go by. Did American men really

wear their hats so differently? *"What else can you tell me about him?"*

"He was older, not very attractive."

"And you still thought it was a tryst?" Penelope asked incredulously.

"Who can understand women? A good-looking, attentive husband at home, and they get bored, take whatever they can find that is different." He shrugged.

"Could it have been something other than a romantic meeting?"

He considered it and shrugged again. *"I don't bother with such details. But I do know she waited until that husband of hers had left, and the cafe, it was not a place she was likely to meet any of her American friends."*

"When was this?"

"The first time was when they were at the hotel. I heard her tell the staff she was off for shopping." A conspiratorial grin came to his face, telling Penelope she was doing anything but that. *"That was why I was surprised to later find her at the cafe...not that I was following her!"*

"Wait...you were the gardener for the hotel as well, correct?"

"I still am," he retorted. *"Though I only maintain it. It is not much work—pruning, weeding—"*

"Fertilizing?" Penelope asked.

"Of course."

"Does your fertilizer use any cyanide as an ingredient?"

His mouth turned down and he studied her. *"If it does, I am not responsible for how others may use it. It isn't as though I keep it in a vault. It's kept in the shed with all the other supplies."*

Penelope chose to interpret that as a yes. She returned to the original topic. *"So you saw Madame Martell meet with this man while she was staying at the hotel, then again more recently?"*

"*I don't snoop,*" he snapped, then relaxed and nodded. *"But yes, that is correct."*

So Finlay had been meeting with an older man in an obscure cafe where she wouldn't have run into anyone she knew. Penelope considered the various possibilities—other than anything romantic. If she was doing it behind George's back, it had to be something he wouldn't have approved of. Was she seeking a divorce? Perhaps she was looking into adopting?

If only Penelope could discover who this mysterious man was. Even with his silly "American" hat, it would be like finding a needle in a haystack.

"Or perhaps someplace more convenient," Penelope said with a growing smile.

CHAPTER TWENTY-FOUR

Penelope had an idea. She wasn't sure how well it would work, but before anything, she needed to eat. By the time she made it back to the villa, it was nearly the lunch hour. She detoured to the kitchen to steal a baguette, butter, and anchovies. She was caught sneaking to the solarium, food in hand.

"There you are."

Penelope nearly dropped everything in surprise. "Goodness Richard, you nearly frightened me to death."

"Frightened you? Everyone has been wondering where you've been all morning. I thought you were going to quickly question the staff and come back."

"I didn't realize I had to check in every hour."

"Of course not. I was just worried is all."

Penelope smiled, relenting. It wasn't so terrible to have someone worried about your welfare, after all. "It simply took longer than I anticipated. And it turned out to be quite fortuitous. I learned some things the Martell's gardener hadn't bothered to tell the police."

Curiosity intervened and Richard's face softened. "What was that?"

Penelope took a moment to set her food down. Richard took the seat across from her. While throwing together her impromptu anchovy sandwich she began by telling him about the separate sleeping arrangements, and how Sara had been in George's "book binding room" during their visit, so she couldn't say if he'd detoured upstairs to get the laudanum in Finlay's room.

She hesitated, continuing to eat before telling him about her adventure to visit Alec. She didn't bother with the details of where he lived and how even the taxi driver had reservations.

"Obviously we have to tell this to the inspector and judge. Something tells me you're right, he probably wasn't as forthcoming with them as he was with you."

"Or...we could find out who this mystery man is so we at least have a name to give them."

Richard gave her a censuring look. "And just how would we do that?"

"I may have glanced at a few old receipts and invoices on George's desk. A certain *advocat* by the name of Edwin Clark was among them. A rather American name, don't you think? The invoice was even kind enough to provide his address here in Antibes."

"And he no doubt handles estates and wills," Richard said dryly. "I don't know what you hope to get from him. I'm not quite fluent in French law, but he'll certainly be bound by privilege under American law."

"Oh, I won't bother with prying into the Martells' private legal matters. But I'm sure he would make time for a wealthy American woman who is seeking legal advice on a delicate estate matter. I may even ask if he knows of a private investigator I could make use of."

Richard sat back to consider that. "Is that who you suspect this mystery man is?"

"I highly doubt it was a paramour. Even if Finlay wasn't seemingly too frail to indulge in that sort of thing, the description alone makes me think he has to be something else. No, I think this was a personal or business matter Finlay wanted handled, obviously without George's knowledge."

"And attorneys are often the ones to put their clients in contact with people who handle such matters."

"Exactly. So, do you think it's safe enough for me to visit an attorney here in Antibes, Detective Prescott?"

"I'm going with you, I don't care how safe it is."

"Naturally."

An hour later, after Penelope had finished eating and freshening up, they told the others they were off on another sleuthing adventure. They were delayed fifteen minutes by Penelope offering the condensed version of her latest news to temporarily satisfy Benny, Lulu, and Cousin Cordelia. They were sated enough to return to the card game they'd been playing.

"One thing I do remember from the invoice on George's desk is the date. It was a month ago," Penelope said to Richard as they were driven to the attorney's office.

"But the most recent will was dated only a week ago."

"Maybe George's surprise wasn't with regard to how quickly the police had obtained the will, but how recently it was dated."

"Perhaps. Again, that's one thing you won't be learning during this visit. Mr. Clark will err on the side of not revealing anything about the Martells at all."

"Oh, I have a plan, don't you worry," Pen said with a slightly smug smile.

"Do I get to know what this plan is?"

"I suppose," she said in a teasing voice before telling him.

Richard nodded in approval. "It's not bad, but be prepared to be disappointed. Either way, we go to the police with everything we've learned."

"Of course, darling."

They arrived at a simple building in a commercial section of town. *Advocat* Edwin Clark had possession of the entire first floor, with a tidy little sign on the front advertising his services—in both English and French. Richard opened the door for her and she entered to find a tiny reception area and a smartly-dressed young woman behind a small reception desk.

"Bonjour," the woman greeted with polite inquiry.

"Bonjour."

Something in their accents must have hinted at being American so she switched to English. "How can I help you?

"I was hoping to briefly meet with Mr. Clark for a short consultation. Though, I'm afraid I don't have an appointment."

The woman pursed her lips at the small faux pas. She studied Richard and Penelope, briefly assessing them. Penelope had made sure to wear her best day dress, something that would reveal just how much she was worth without her having to say it. Apparently, it was enough as the woman quickly consulted the appointment book in front of her.

"Please have a seat while I see if Monsieur Clark has a moment. May I have your names, *s'il vous plaît?*"

After giving her their names, she disappeared behind a door. When she returned she sported a smile.

"If you please, Monsieur Clark has a *brief* window."

They rose and thanked her, walking past the door she held open and into Mr. Clark's office. The receptionist gently closed the door behind them.

Edwin Clark was much younger than Penelope expected. Her experience with attorneys had been mostly the elderly veterans who had serviced generations of wealthy New York families. Mr. Clark looked to be in his mid-thirties, with a spry look, a modern suit, and a more casual air.

"Good morning! I understand you need a brief consultation? Marie told me you were Americans. She's usually good about sussing out that sort of thing, I hope you don't mind. Rest assured, I'm perfectly licensed to practice here in France as well as in several American states. It's what I specialize in, negotiating these tricky intercontinental situations. My mother is French, born and raised."

"How convenient," Pen said as she and Richard took the two seats in the office.

"Yes, yes, what with so many Americans moving to the Côte d'Azur, I hopped aboard the S.S. France and here I am," he said cheerfully, pleased at his own ingenuity. "It's turned out to be quite the boon."

"I'm pleased to hear that. Hopefully, that means you'll be able to help me."

He allowed the cheerful look on his face to relax into something more professionally neutral. "Yes, of course. What can I do for you two today?"

"Sadly, I've come to you because of Mrs. Finlay Martell," Penelope said in a somber tone.

A guarded look came to Mr. Clark's face. "Yes, that was terrible news, just terrible." He hesitated before continuing.

"Of course, I'm not at liberty to discuss other clients, even after death."

"Oh, of course! I should have made myself clear," Penelope quickly said, pretending that she hadn't meant to make it seem that way at all. In her periphery, she could see Richard biting back a smile at her little test. Sadly, Mr. Clark *was* a conscientious attorney. "However, before she… passed, Finlay told me you had recommended a man to her, someone who could help me with a delicate matter of my own. Unfortunately, I've completely forgotten his name. She did mention his hat had a striped band. I know it's such a silly and minor thing to remark upon, and may not be all that helpful, but…."

"That sounds like Adam Nohelty." Mr. Clark's brow was wrinkled in confusion. "And you say Mrs. Martell suggested him to you?"

"She thought I might avail myself of his services."

"Well," his brow rose and fell in acknowledgment, "Yes, he is a good private investigator. I wouldn't have recommended him, otherwise."

Penelope's plan had worked even better than expected. As predicted, this Mr. Nohelty was a private investigator. Even if they didn't get any information from him, they could at least go to the police with a name.

"I would put you in touch with him, but I'm afraid he's back in the good old U.S.A."

"He is?" Penelope hadn't been expecting that.

"Yes, I suppose Mrs. Martell didn't have an opportunity to tell you as much before she…"

"No, I suppose not," Pen said, feeling deflated. She wondered just how far she could pry before Mr. Clark sent them packing. "I suppose she hired him in relation to her desire to adopt."

There was a brief flash of surprise in his eyes, which he quickly masked. "I'm afraid I couldn't say. Nor, could Mr. Nohelty," he added with a censuring tone in his voice.

"I would expect not."

Mr. Clark leaned over his desk and gave them both penetrating looks, particularly Penelope. "I have the oddest sensation that it isn't a legal consultation you two are after. In fact, I find it particularly unseemly that you would take advantage of my time and connection to poor Mrs. Martell to satisfy some bit of morbid curiosity for the sake of gossip."

Penelope felt the need to defend them both. "I'm not prying for the sake of gossip, Mr. Clark. We're trying to find out what really happened to Finlay. I'm actually a private investigator myself and Mr. Prescott here is a detective with the New York Police Department."

"But certainly not acting in any official capacity," Richard said, giving Penelope a quick warning glance. "I'm afraid we have overstepped and I offer our apologies. We won't bother you any further."

He stood up, which meant Penelope had to as well. At any rate, there was nothing more to learn, as Mr. Clark had caught on to her little scheme. They saw themselves out.

"I suppose you deserve some bit of commendation for trying," Richard said once they were outside again, the door firmly closed behind them.

"You have to admit it worked. We know that it was in fact a private detective that Finlay was speaking to. We also got a name. And did you see his reaction when I suggested she was adopting a child?"

"I did, though it doesn't necessarily mean you were correct in that assessment." Richard rubbed his chin in thought. "Odd, that it would all be done in secret. Unless she was also planning to divorce George, Finlay wouldn't have been able to adopt without his consent."

"Perhaps she was killing two birds with one stone. It certainly creates motive. Did George learn of her plans?"

"We're doing a lot of supposition here. Frankly, without more information from Mr. Clark or Mr. Nohelty, that's all it is. We don't have proof of anything. However, we do have enough to take to the police, who will have more resources and legal avenues at their disposal."

"Yes, yes," Pen said in resignation.

Richard smiled. "Don't look so disappointed. You did good today, better than many a detective would have. You may have even dug up enough for the police to put everything into place to solve this murder."

"Do you think? Of course, that's only Finlay's murder. There is still Vera's. How can we learn more about that one?"

"A better question is, didn't we come here to relax? Get away from this sort of thing?"

"Richard, a murderer is on the loose," Pen admonished. "As you suggested earlier, I can hardly relax knowing he or she has yet to be caught."

"I suppose I deserve that," he said with a wry smile.

"Oh don't be so sour," Pen said cozying into him. "I'm only suggesting we pay a visit to the hotel to see how Prynne and Lily are doing."

"And who knows? we may even get a confession," he teased.

"That, we may."

CHAPTER TWENTY-FIVE

P enelope persuaded Richard to visit the Hôtel de Platine before going to the Commissariat about what they'd learned from Mr. Clark. She thought they might learn more that would be helpful in the investigation, and it was better to make one trip to the police than two.

The hotel seemed inappropriately bright, glowing in the afternoon sun. The white facade had an ironically inviting appeal that actually worked well for its future as a luxury hotel, rather than the de facto foreign home of American expats.

Penelope wondered what would become of the hotel now, especially since renovations had presumably ceased for the time being.

They were greeted by Julia, who met them at the front doors. It seemed she was continuing her service to the Tynehook sisters in the wake of their mother's death, perhaps long enough to handle their affairs. Or, as she'd revealed in the bar the night before, she truly cared about them.

"Miss Banks, Mr. Prescott. Good afternoon." She didn't

open the door wider or show any indication of welcoming them in.

"It occurred to me that I had yet to offer my official condolences, and—"

"I'm afraid the Tynehook family is not seeing anyone at present."

"It's alright, Julia," Prynne's soft voice said from somewhere further inside.

Julia's mouth tightened with disapproval and she hesitated before opening the door wider for them. The foyer felt much larger without guests to fill it. It was darker and seemed haunted by the ghost of Vera. Pen's eyes inadvertently darted to the spot where she had breathed her last breath. The chairs and small table were gone.

Despite the lingering trace of grief on her face, Prynne seemed to be bearing her mother's death rather well. Her cheeks were a healthy shade of pink and she'd gotten a bit of sun, if the glow to her skin was any indication.

Still, she greeted them with a wan smile. "It's so kind of you to come by, Miss Banks, Mr. Prescott."

"We simply came to offer our condolences, Miss Tynehook," Richard said.

"If there is anything you need, please let us know." Penelope looked around again.

"Lily and I are moving out of this hotel. I simply couldn't stay here, after..." Her eyes slid to the place where her mother had died.

"Of course, that's perfectly understandable." Penelope paused for a brief moment. "What do you plan on doing with the hotel? I assume it's been left to you and your sister?"

"Only me," Prynne said, oddly angry about that.

"Mother always made it quite clear the rules under which Lily would inherit."

"Those are matters which you needn't worry yourself about at present," Julia said, giving Penelope and Richard a hard glance.

"I didn't mean to upset you. I arrived too late to Antibes to have visited the hotel before your mother bought it. I've only really seen the foyer. The grounds look quite lovely," Pen said, eyeing the French doors that led to the garden at the back of the property.

"Oh, it is lovely!" Prynne said, brightening up. "I'd be happy to give you a tour of the best features."

"Prynne, I think—"

"It's fine, Julia. It will take my mind off...everything." Before Julia could object further, Prynne led them through the French doors.

Penelope was glad her not-so-subtle suggestion had been fruitful. All the better if it did take Prynne's mind off her mother's death. The flowers in the large garden had mostly lost their bloom, though the same peonies from the Martell's home were on display.

"You should have seen it when we first came, especially in the spring. It was bursting with color. And the mural, well..." Prynne turned to look at a wall to the side, which was mostly a stark white. The painters hadn't finished covering it—perhaps casualties of the curse over the hotel. Pen could still see a colorfully vivid garden that would last all year long. Or at least it would have if not for Vera's intervention. No wonder Finlay had been so upset, it was quite lovely.

Prynne walked them further on toward the landing that led to the rocky cliffs along the shore.

"It's a lovely view from here, though it is a shame there

isn't much beach access. Mother didn't care much about that. The idea of guests tracking in sand and salt water didn't sit well with her."

"Did your mother have designs on this hotel prior to arriving in Antibes?"

Prynne didn't answer right away, instead staring out at the water with a troubled look. "I don't know why she bought this hotel, to tell you the truth. I...I really shouldn't speak ill of her, especially now, but I had the feeling the purchase was out of spite. She took issue with the Martells from the moment we first arrived. She made it her mission to buy this hotel once she knew they had designs on buying it themselves. This was all meant to be a fun holiday for Lily, prior to..." Prynne exhaled and turned to them with a tight smile. "I suppose Lily has every reason to break her engagement now. That's one good thing, at least. I thought it unfair, Mother practically forcing her into this marriage. But she's had a near obsession with the British aristocracy as long as I can remember. Americans are so uncouth, she'd always say." Prynne sighed, as though the residual weariness of her mother's opinions still lingered.

"How is Lily?" Penelope asked.

"She went on another of her usual early morning disappearances, so I assume she is doing well. She likes to bring back lavender each morning for me. She knows how much I adore it, though I have no idea how she bought it. Mother certainly never gave either of us any money to spend so frivolously." She frowned slightly. "She's been gone longer than usual today. She's far more independent than I am. I honestly don't know what to do with myself without Mother dictating every—" Prynne stopped, her cheeks coloring with embarrassment at how much she had inadvertently revealed.

"We certainly aren't judging, Prynne. It's a difficult thing losing someone you've spent most of your life with, especially a parent. Even those who are a bit controlling. I have some experience with that myself."

"Mother wasn't terrible," Prynne quickly said. "She was just concerned about me, that's all. I was so sick as a child, she spent all her time caring for me. Then, after my father died, she had to take care of his business affairs. It wasn't easy for her, especially as a woman. Yes, she had Julia and I had a nurse, but she felt I needed a familial touch in her absence. I suppose it finally occurred to her that I had never played with other children and didn't have any siblings or cousins. And poor Lily needed someone as well, her parents having just died in that horrid car accident. I suppose there was something to that. I became healthier, though I was never hale and hearty again. It worked out well for both of us. At least until Lily... matured. She's beautiful, and could have had any man she wanted, even before Mother intervened with all her *improvements*." Prynne blushed slightly, and Pen wondered if she was thinking of Peter. "I'm not like Lily. She's so...different. She was always meant to be someone special, oddly enough because Mother began treating her that way. In many ways, she had it much, much worse than me. She wanted to go to Broadway to become an actress. Mother was, of course, appalled at the idea. She told her she would buy any theater Lily dared to audition at. Her method of getting her way was throwing money at things until someone was so backed into a corner, they had no choice but to abide. Or in Lily's case, threatening to take it away." Prynne looked out at the water with a troubled expression.

Penelope and Richard eyed each other, wondering how

long they should wait before speaking. Fortunately, Prynne perked up, flashing a smile.

"Would you like to see one of the rooms? I suppose I could show you the suite Mother and I shared. It's the only one that's been fully redone in the way Mother planned. One thing I can say about my mother is that she did have an eye for design and a head for business."

"Of course," Penelope said brightly.

Prynne smiled again and walked back toward the garden. "I'll take you in the back way. The rear stairs were my usual venue of escape. I tended to stay in the back gardens or that overlook. It's as close to the sea as I've been allowed to get since I arrived. I suppose now..." She stopped and stared thoughtfully at the ground.

"There is no shame in having conflicting emotions, Prynne," Penelope said gently. "Being glad of one bit of freedom doesn't mean you're happy about what happened to your mother."

Prynne nodded and flashed another forced smile their way. "Yes, of course. It actually seems rather selfish when George has lost poor Finlay. I still can't believe that he killed her. Finlay was so sweet to Lily and me, and George seemed so charming and doting." Her smile faded. "Sadly, I suppose an overly attentive husband can often mask his true intentions."

"Very true," Richard said somberly. "Most murders are committed by individuals closest to the victim."

"Especially in the case of wives and their husbands, as my fiancé has made sure to remind me," Pen said, earning herself a wry look from Richard.

Prynne smiled and led them on. They passed a small shed abutting the garden. It was mostly camouflaged by bushes and trees, and there was a sign indicating it was for staff only. That must have been where Alec kept the gardening supplies, including any fertilizer. There was a keyhole, which meant it was kept locked. Surely, Vera would have had a key to every door in the hotel, including that one. Thus, anyone close to her would have also had access. The same people who'd had access to her drink the night of the murder.

"Please ignore the mess we're about to pass," Prynne said as they continued. "So many of the workmen quit during the renovations and Mother, or rather Julia, was unable to find someone willing to even remove the debris. But I suppose it offers a small, if sadly tragic, picture of what the hotel once looked like."

They passed by bins overflowing with the detritus of the renovation project: timber, paint cans, pipes, and wallpaper.

"That's the same wallpaper in the Martell's home," Penelope pointed out, coming to a stop.

"It is," Richard agreed. His brow furrowed and he turned to Prynne. "You mentioned that you shared a suite with your mother. Was this wallpaper there when you first moved in?"

"Yes, why?"

"And Lily had her own suite, I presume?"

Prynne nodded. "Right across the hall."

"I assume that suite didn't have the same wallpaper?"

"No, it didn't. I don't understand what this has to do with anything."

Richard was already looking at Penelope, who had just arrived at the same conclusion he had. She turned to Prynne, who still wore an expression of utter confusion.

"My friends, Benjamin Davenport and Cousin Cordelia, they told me last night that you and your mother were quite sick when you first moved in. That you eventually overcame it. Was that after the wallpaper was removed?"

Prynne thought about it, and after a moment, her eyes widened. "Mostly Mother, she certainly had the worst of it. But...surely you don't think it was the wallpaper? It couldn't have been. Both George and Finlay would have been sick as well."

"Except only *one* of them seems to have been suffering a long term ailment of some unknown cause," Penelope said.

"At least until yesterday," Richard corrected. He turned to the wallpaper. "And now, I suppose we know why."

CHAPTER TWENTY-SIX

Richard had called the police and Inspector Cloutier had arrived. The area with the debris, including the wallpaper, had been sectioned off. A sample of the wallpaper had already been carefully removed and sent for testing to confirm the presence of anything that might cause illness. The most likely culprit was arsenic. Penelope worried about how much arsenic she'd been exposed to during that visit in the Martell's sunroom, as brief as it was.

All of them were presently in the suite that Prynne had shared with her mother. It was impressively spacious, with two bedrooms, two bathrooms, a sitting room and a small office. One bedroom was noticeably larger, which Vera must have made her own, delegating the smaller one to Prynne.

"Only the larger bedroom had the wallpaper," Prynne said. "I shudder to think what may have happened to Mother had she not taken an instant dislike to it. Her stubbornness may have saved her life."

"But you suffered the same symptoms, no? Even though your room didn't have the wallpaper?" Penelope asked, earning her an irritated glance from the inspector.

"I usually spent most of my time with Mother. She was so ill at the time, I spent nearly all day by her side while she lay in bed. I suppose that's also what caused poor Finlay to be so sickly, having the same wallpaper in her room. Of course, she probably started off healthier than me, and certainly younger than Mother. Even Julia became somewhat ill, coming into Mother's room every so often to consult her on some matter. We almost failed to have the wallpaper removed, as she could barely make it to the sitting room. But she was loath to halt any renovations, even while suffering so. She claimed it wreaked havoc with her sensibilities."

"And no one made the connection to the wallpaper once it was removed?" Inspector Cloutier asked.

Prynne shook her head. "Mother insisted it was some exotic Mediterranean affliction. Even the doctor she privately consulted with couldn't determine what the cause was."

"No?" Inspector Cloutier frowned. "I would have thought a medical professional would know the symptoms of arsenic poison. Do you have a name for this doctor?"

Prynne's brow rose in thought, then she shook her head. "Offhand, no. But Julia would know. She handled such matters. She's in town handling our mother's affairs at the moment."

Inspector Cloutier nodded. "I've instructed one of my officers to have her sent up when she returns."

"How could the arsenic in Mrs. Tynehook's drink have come from the wallpaper?" Pen asked Inspector Cloutier.

"Perhaps if it were turned into a fine dust? However, the amount in Madame Tynehook's glass was quite substantial."

"Such that a small segment of wallpaper might not have been enough?" Richard asked.

"We will have to test it to be sure."

"But ultimately it was the cyanide that..." Penelope refrained from mentioning Vera's death for Prynne's sake.

"*Oui*," Inspector Cloutier confirmed. "That was the official cause of death."

"Is it possible to know the source of it?"

The inspector shook his head. "If we had a sample of the original, perhaps. But cyanide is surprisingly common in many household materials."

"Like gardening, it's used in fertilizer. There is a small shed near the back garden here. You might check there. A man named Alec, he was the gardener for the hotel. He also worked for the Martells." Penelope said.

All eyes turned to Prynne, whose own had widened with familiarity. "Yes, that's true. I only met him in passing, of course, during my many ventures to the garden."

"I imagine he used the same fertilizer in both places," Richard said.

Inspector Cloutier nodded. "We will speak with him again."

Prynne brought a hand up to her cheek. "My goodness, so many ways one can die simply from the little pleasures in life."

Penelope had to agree that it was rather alarming, the many ways one's environment could kill a person. Things that may have been deemed perfectly safe a hundred or even ten years ago were now discovered to be deadly. Even medicine itself was constantly evolving. The doctor Mrs. Tynehook had hired hadn't even been able to uncover the cause of her ailment. Apparently, neither had Finlay's.

"Dr. Archambault."

All eyes now turned to Penelope, most filled with surprise. Richard's, of course, wasn't. He was used to her sudden sparks of remembrance.

"I'm certain he was Finlay's doctor. A Doctor Hugo Archambault."

Inspector Cloutier regarded her with some suspicion. "How do you know this?"

"I saw it in passing on an invoice when I visited the Martell home."

"Hmm." The inspector nodded. "I will be looking into this doctor."

There was a knock on the door to the suite, and Julia entered. The look of curiosity on her face was understandable, though it was slightly overshadowed by the obvious concern for Prynne.

"I was told by one of the officers downstairs that you wanted to speak with me?" Julia said, shifting her attention from Prynne to Inspector Cloutier.

"*Oui*," Inspector Cloutier said, gesturing for her to enter and join them.

Her eyes flitted with wary regard to Penelope and Richard before she fully turned her attention to the inspector. "How may I help you?"

"The doctor you procured for Madame Tynehook during her period of illness, what was the name, s'il vous plaît?"

She paused to consider it. "I believe his name was Dr. Breguet, Cedric Breguet."

So, there was no connection there, after all. What would a connection between shared doctors have led to? The same negligence in failing to determine what was making Finlay, Vera, and Prynne so ill?

"And do you know what was discussed during her visit with this doctor?"

"Of course not. She met with him in private."

A brief look of irritation flashed across Inspector Cloutier's face. "Do you know if this doctor found a cause for Madame Tynehook's illness?"

"If so, she did not tell me."

"And the wallpaper, how soon was it removed after this visit with the doctor? Did she, er...accelerate the removal?"

Julia's brow furrowed, no doubt from wondering what that had to do with anything. "She had always intended to have it removed. As far as I could tell, it seemed no more or less urgent after the visit. She simply wanted the renovations to the suite over and done with so she could recover in the privacy and peace of her own room without distraction."

"I see."

Yes, it was a good thing, for both Vera and Prynne, that Vera had taken such a dislike to the wallpaper. Sadly, Finlay had only grown to admire it.

"If you could remain here please, I would like to question you further." Inspector Cloutier turned to Penelope and Richard. "You have both been quite helpful, but I will no longer require your presence."

Penelope was dismayed by the glaring dismissal but understood. She followed Richard out of the suite and out of the hotel. They walked for a bit, enjoying the fine weather.

"It's odd that two doctors would miss the symptoms of arsenic poisoning, don't you think?"

"Odd, but not inherently suspicious. It's uncommon enough that it might not be an obvious diagnosis." Richard eyed her, a knowing smile on his face. "If you're hoping to get any information from either doctor using your prior prank with Mr. Clark, you'll find the same obstacle. I'd say the inspector himself would be lucky to get any information."

"It wasn't a prank, it was...good investigating."

Richard smiled and pulled her into his side. "I suppose."

Penelope allowed herself to sink into Richard, enjoying the feel of him. "So many people ill, and all because of some old wallpaper."

"Arsenic was quite common as an agent in pigment, once upon a time. I probably should have realized it earlier, what with the art courses I took at Princeton. But those classes focused mostly on the results, not the process of creating art."

"Don't feel too badly about it, darling. Who would have thought arsenic would even be a common ingredient in wallpaper?"

"Someone who knows the history of dyes and pigments. It's a wonder humans have survived as long as we have, considering the numerous ways we've inadvertently found to kill ourselves via everyday activities like decoration, clothing, even—"

"Reading!" Penelope said, pulling away and standing erect. "George was a bookbinder. All those dyed leathers and glues and who knows what else? He must have known about the wallpaper."

Richard considered it with a grim expression. "Yes, he should have. Do you think it was deliberate, the choice of wallpaper?"

"Finlay did suggest he'd been the one to choose it. That, and any dyes from binding the books she was surrounded by daily. It's a wonder it didn't have the same violent effects on Finlay, even if she was younger and healthier than the

Tynehooks. I'm still horrified to think what we were exposed to just from our visit!"

"Yes," Richard said angrily, pulling her in closer to his side as though to protect her retroactively. "George did try to get us to move the visit to the parlor. He must have worried about it himself."

"Because he knew," Penelope said, angry on Finlay's behalf. "I wonder if Finlay eventually did as well. Perhaps that was her motive for framing him, as well as killing herself. Maybe the effects had finally reached the point where she knew she'd never recover. Oh, how I wish I could force this doctor of hers to speak."

"The good news is, an autopsy would say for sure. The difficult part is proving that George deliberately poisoned her."

"And why? It seemingly started before she fully came into her inheritance."

"People react differently, and it's possible she could have built up a small immunity such that the effects took longer to present."

"Perhaps, but as you said, it would be difficult to prove. Now that we know it began before she even came into control of her inheritance, it will also be difficult to prove motive." Penelope considered all the pieces to this puzzle, trying to glean a connection that would lead to an answer. For some reason, it was still a jumbled mess in her head. She was oddly hungry yet again and blamed that on her sleuthing skills not being quite up to par. "Let's go home, perhaps the others will help shake loose a clue that cinches the case."

CHAPTER TWENTY-SEVEN

Berthe had made some small sandwiches, pastries, and cookies for an afternoon tea at the villa. While the five occupants of the house enjoyed the selections in the solarium, Penelope and Richard told them of their discoveries that day.

"Thank goodness green has never suited me," Benny said, hand pressed to his chest. "I've always favored purple."

"Or violet?" Pen teased, thinking of a prior case they'd worked on together.

He pursed his lips. "Leave the tartness to the lemon-mouths, Pen."

"Speaking of lemon-mouths, I'll have to ask Berthe to buy more ginger ale. I don't think I'm inclined to drink any lemonade for a long while after today."

"George really was trying to slowly kill her, it seems," Cousin Cordelia said in horror.

"But was he the one to try and finish the job at the party?" Lulu asked.

"Or at their house while we were there?" Penelope added.

"If it wasn't about the inheritance, which she had yet to get a hold of, what could it have been about?" Benny asked.

"Hmm," Richard hummed in thought, finishing his bite of a pâté sandwich. "One of the side effects of arsenic poisoning is the loss or prevention of a pregnancy. Perhaps George was ensuring his own future inheritance."

"Goodness, what an awful man!" Cousin Cordelia gasped.

"Agreed," Lulu said.

Penelope's thoughts mimicked both of theirs.

"But once Finlay began making noise about adoption, he decided he had to finally secure it for good," Penelope said. "All the more so, now that she had her inheritance. In fact, now that I think about it...the will."

"What about it?" Richard asked.

"Remember when we met with George at the Commissariat? He was surprised about the will being discovered so soon. What if that isn't what he was referring to? What if he was simply surprised that Finlay had updated it so recently?"

"But what did she change?"

"It had to be something about the children. She must have added a clause in there about adoption, no doubt in preparation for adopting."

"But he was surprised. If he had no idea she'd updated the will, that couldn't speak to motive."

"Perhaps he was acting off the old will, in which they were still waiting to start a family the natural way. He wanted her out of the way before either that happened, despite his best efforts, or she adopted with or without him."

"You mean divorce?"

Pen nodded.

"And when it didn't work at Vera's party, he tried again with something else at home," Lulu said.

"He certainly plays the gigalo when it comes to poisons. He wasn't picky about which one he chose. Also, if it was to avoid detection, you'd have thought he'd be less public about using them."

"True, it doesn't make sense to practically point the finger at himself both at Vera's party, then in front of the two of you."

Penelope and Richard eyed one another. They had kept true to their promise not to tell anyone that there'd been two forms of poison in Vera's drink.

"I'm sure the judge only meant for us not to tell anyone who was a likely suspect. Certainly we can trust our own friends," Penelope pleaded.

"Trust us with what?" Benny asked.

Richard exhaled. "I suppose now the cat is out of the bag, though you're probably right, my dear."

"Tell us what?" Benny insisted.

"There were two forms of poison in Vera's glass the night of the party, arsenic and cyanide," Richard confessed.

"This is *strictly confidential*," Penelope added over the sounds of their reactions.

"So either someone really wanted Vera dead, or there are two suspects in her murder," Benny said.

"Or both Finlay and Vera were the targets," Lulu surmised.

"That's what I think is the case," Penelope said. "Especially with everything we now know. George is, of course, the most obvious suspect for one of those poisons."

"But again, why try so publicly, both times?"

"Witnesses? Perhaps he was hoping the audacity of

doing it in front of others might make him seem innocent. Who would be that bold?" Benny offered.

"The real problem is, all of this is circumstantial. Even the slow poisoning of Finlay long before the murders. She was the one who told us green was her favorite color. I'd be willing to bet she was also the one to pay for that wallpaper, even if George was the one to suggest it. You'll never get him to admit to it, now that she's dead. And if there's any arsenic or other poison in that book binding room of his, it's gone now. We have no proof to speak of."

"No, I suppose we don't," Penelope said with a sigh of disappointment.

She couldn't help but picture that scene from the sunroom in vivid color in her head. Knowing what she did about Finlay's exposure to so much arsenic, it was a wonder she'd been such a gracious hostess. Smiling and chatting through it all.

"Leslie Chambers!" Penelope suddenly exclaimed, perking up as something occurred to her.

"Who is Leslie Chambers?" Richard asked.

"An odious little tyrant I would have rather not been reminded of," Benny said, the sides of his mouth turned down.

"Not him, per se, but I recall one little prank of his in particular."

"Only one?" Benny groused, an eyebrow arched. "I seem to recall him having a fine time tormenting any creature unfortunate enough to cross his path."

"Care to tell me what this man—or boy?—has to do with either case?"

"Really, every child is guilty of it, myself included," Pen said, standing up and pacing the floor. She stopped and turned to Richard. "One of the things that's been sticky in this case is how anyone other than George could have gotten the laudanum into Finlay's glass."

"Yes," Richard said, urging her to continue.

"And the empty bottle was right there in plain sight on her nightstand, where George surely knew it would be, or would have at least seen it."

"I assume that's why the police arrested him," Benny said dryly.

"What if that's what Finlay wanted?"

"What does all of this have to do with this Leslie Chambers?" Richard asked.

"It was at Stella Cox's birthday party. I was seven at the time, wearing a pretty white dress with a blue sash. Red punch was served. That little devil drank nearly a cupful, kept it in his mouth, then ran right up to me and..."

"Clapped both of his cheeks," Richard finished, grinning in understanding. Apparently, the prank was universal among children the world over. "I imagine that dress wasn't so white after the fact."

"No, it wasn't," Pen said, still bitter about it.

"But you make a good point. When Finlay returned after changing, she didn't say anything before sipping her lemonade. She *could* have had the laudanum in her mouth and simply spit it into the drink as soon as she brought it up to supposedly take a sip."

"Exactly."

"Gives new meaning to the term femme fatale," Benny quipped.

"But that just gets us back to the question of why Finlay would kill herself," Richard said. "And why now?"

"Maybe the illness was too much? Maybe she finally discovered what George had been doing with the wallpaper and books and flowers and who knows what else? Framing him for her own murder, it's extreme, but surely you've seen worse in your job?"

"I've seen people killed over a bit of spilled beer, but that usually falls under fits of passion. To be this meticulous and deliberate about it? You'd really need to have solid evidence just to get it to court."

"Sadly, I don't think it needs to be proven that Finlay killed herself, George just needs a plausible theory as to how and why he didn't do it. I'm pretty sure the French have some equivalent standard to our own reasonable doubt before finding someone guilty. And I've just thought of one for him."

"But are you going to tell the police?" Benny asked.

Penelope and Richard looked at one another.

"Justice works both ways, my dear," Richard said. "Unfortunately, your theory makes more sense than George boldly poisoning her in front of us."

"It also makes sense when you consider the party. Maybe she wanted to frame him there as well, but Vera's murder was a more compelling draw."

"Little did she know she wasn't the only one with that goal in mind."

"True," Penelope said, feeling exhausted.

Richard must have noted her fatigue. "Let's forget about murder for a while and enjoy our afternoon tea."

Penelope certainly wasn't going to complain. The warmth of sunshine and the lovely view were enough to help her forget about Vera and Finlay.

"It really is nice here. I missed Antibes on all my prior visits to France," Penelope said, admiring the view through the large windows.

"I'm afraid the entire Riviera wasn't a part of my tour during the war, or after the fact."

Penelope turned to study Richard. "Some of your war buddies are still in Paris, you said. I can't wait to meet them."

A strange smile came to his face. "Yes, that should be...interesting. I'll be curious myself to see how some of them are getting on. It was easy to get lost in that city, start over, as though your prior life never even existed. I almost fell prey to it myself. Going home, especially with everything that happened with Franklin—Franky—and then Sophie and my brother. Being in Paris made me feel like one of the lotus eaters. That's not living, that's...escaping."

"Well, I'm glad you came home," Pen said, reaching her hand across to place on his.

His eyes flicked back to her and he grinned. "I am too. After all, if not for you, I wouldn't be here enjoying a delicious ham sandwich, looking at this gorgeous view, and... smelling the foulest stench of anchovies—"

Penelope laughed and kicked him under the table. "I'll try to limit them from now on."

"Thank goodness for that!" Benny said with a laugh. Lulu lifted her cup in agreement.

Penelope pursed her lips. "Besides, I can see France is already beginning to have an impact on my waistline. I may have to go for longer walks in the morning," she said as she turned to look out at the small garden again.

"I suppose I'll have to wake up earlier to accompany you."

"Oh for heaven's sake, Richard," Pen laughed. "It isn't Jack the Ripper terrorizing the streets of Antibes. I'll be perfectly fine buying flowers and baguettes and pressuring the occasional shop owner into opening early to..."

Richard stared at her. "That's quite the pause. Should I

be worried about what my fiancée is doing with these shop owners?"

No...I..." Penelope's brow wrinkled as things started falling into place in her head. Suddenly her eyes widened and she stared back at Richard. "I can't believe it!"

"Can't believe what?"

"It was all there from the very beginning. I think I've figured it out!"

CHAPTER TWENTY-EIGHT

"What is it you've figured out?" Lulu asked Penelope.

"It was something Estelle said when I ran into her during my morning walk a few days ago. She told me that George habitually bought flowers early in the morning for Finlay. With everything I now know, that doesn't make any sense."

"A man buying flowers for his wife? That makes perfect sense, Penelope. Well, perhaps not for one who wishes her dead, but under normal circumstances, surely?" Cousin Cordelia said.

"Yes, under normal circumstances," Pen agreed. "But this is hardly normal. Still, he *was* buying flowers, at least according to Estelle. But there are several problems with that."

"Which is?" Benny asked.

"Well, for one, when Richard and I went to the Martell's home, George had a difficult time finding a vase."

"Maybe the only available vases were being used for the flowers he'd bought her?" Lulu suggested.

"We didn't see any in the house. Surely they'd be on display, or we might have smelled them? And in her room, Finlay had only silk flowers. She even referred to the lavender we'd brought as a 'rare treat.'"

"Oh, get to it already, who was he buying flowers for? It was Estelle wasn't it?" Benny said.

"No, not her. She wouldn't have mentioned his buying flowers at all if they'd secretly been for her."

"Well don't keep us in suspense, Pen, who were they for?" Lulu asked.

"Lily."

The confused looks that ensued were expected.

"When I first saw Lily that morning, walking with Estelle, she had a bunch of lavender in her hands. I thought it had come from Marc, the man she was with—young love and all. Then, Prynne mentioned that Lily brings back lavender for her almost every morning. That seems too much of an expense for a young man struggling to support his mother and sister. So, perhaps Lily was buying it herself? No. I was told she never received even a small bit of spending money. Lavender isn't cheap, even in American dollars. However, with no money, how did she afford it? And almost every morning? She wouldn't, not unless someone else was buying them for her."

"So you think George was having a secret tryst with Lily?" Benny asked, eyes aglitter at this tidbit.

"You saw her the night of the wake. It wasn't for Finlay's sake that she was upset. She was upset about *him* being arrested."

"You would have thought she'd be happy Finlay was out of the way, if she was truly interested in George," Lulu said.

"Perhaps she was only interested in him for the

moment. A little dalliance before being trapped in marriage," Benny offered.

Penelope considered that, replaying Lily's protest in her head. "Perhaps she thought it unnecessary for him to murder her. Maybe George oversold just how sick she was, hinted that she would be dead long before Lily would be forced into marriage?"

"Oh, that devil!" Cousin Cordelia spat.

"Indeed, and a devil with poor judgment at that," Benny said. "Vera would have never given Lily money had she run off with him. Surely, even he would have known that."

"Perhaps he really liked the girl? Was willing to give it all up to run off with her?" Lulu said, her voice dripping with sarcasm.

"No, that one is mercenary," Penelope said. "It's the very reason he's been slowly poisoning his wife. He's after money. He was simply biding his time until his slow poisoning of his wife accomplished the deed."

"You know, this very likely means Lily was the one to add one of the doses of poison," Benny said.

"Yes," Pen said with a sigh, not liking that fact.

"Once again, I have to remind everyone about the tricky problem of evidence," Richard said. "Estelle's observation that George bought flowers each morning is hardly conclusive on its own, especially now that Finlay isn't alive to refute it."

"Surely the staff could," Pen said. Even Sara, who seemed so smitten with Monsieur wouldn't go so far as to lie to the police.

"That would only prove that the flowers weren't going to his wife, not that they were going to Lily."

"So how do we prove it?" Lulu asked.

"By going to someone else who has an ear for gossip, if only by virtue of his trade. The bartender," Penelope said.

This time around, Penelope had no qualms about taking Benny with her. Benny was just as fluent in French as she was. They had asked around and there was only one grocer that was open early enough for Marc to have been dressed for work at the same time Pen and Estelle had caught him conversing with Lily that morning. Inspector Cloutier had suggested he might be released, so she had her fingers crossed that he not only would be, but that his employer wouldn't have fired him in the meantime.

She was happy to find him stocking the back room of the grocery store. He paused upon exiting into the main store area and seeing the two of them staring at him.

"What is this?" Marc asked in French.

"We're here to ask about what you saw during your morning trysts with Lily," Benny quickly blurted before Penelope could say anything. She shot him an exasperated look.

Marc narrowed his eyes and wordlessly bent down to pick up another box of food to take back. Pen sighed when he disappeared into the back.

"Zounds, Benny!"

"I thought, why not get straight to the point?"

When Marc reappeared to get more food to take back, he deliberately ignored them.

"Marc—"

He disappeared into the back with the last crate before she could finish. They waited for him to return, but it seemed he intended to remain back there until they left.

Oh, pineapples!" Penelope huffed. She pushed past the door, grimacing at the layer of dirt left on her hand. Marc spun to face her in surprise and outrage. She blurted out her question before he could protest.

"*Did you ever see George Martell and Lily Tynehook together?*"

Marc paused to study her, debating whether to respond this time. He muttered a curse and his eyes darted past her toward the swinging door, wondering if anyone was listening. When they eventually landed back on Penelope, they were filled with sardonic amusement.

"*Outside.*"

Penelope followed him back through the store, making sure not to touch the door with her hands again. She and Benny then followed him into the street. He led them far enough from the entrance of the shop that the owner wouldn't hear or see him.

"*I come here to help open the shop in the morning. I would see both of them, not together. At least not at first.*"

"*And then?*" Benny urged.

"And then..." he began in English, a subtle smile coming to his face, "I followed—*the girl, not the man*," he finished quickly in French.

"Naturellement," Benny lamented.

"*There is only one flower shop open so early. I saw her with the flowers. I put it together. In the beginning, I thought I would meet her there. Perhaps buy her a small flower of appreciation to see if she would entertain something with me.*" The rakish smile that came to his face was quickly snuffed out by a look of resignation. "*I saw the man she was getting her flowers from—always lavender. It was the same man I saw at the party with Madame Martell. Then, I confront—the girl, not the man.*"

"*And what did Lily have to say about it?*" Pen asked.

"*She denied it of course. It was not my business, so I left it. But I know she is from the hotel. I think, 'maybe she can help me, ah, forget what I know.'*" He tapped his forehead.

"Well now, aren't you clever," Benny purred. Marc gave him an uncertain look.

"*That's when she got you the job as the bartender.*"

He simply nodded, but there was a guarded look on his face, as though that wasn't the entirety of Lily's offer.

"The curse!"

Both Marc and Benny started at Penelope's exclamation. Marc was the one who didn't seem confused.

"*That's what she wanted you to do. Sabotage the progress of the renovations, no?*"

He frowned looking off to the side in regret. "*I did not understand it. At first, I thought it was a trap. Then, when I saw how much she would be paying....*" He shrugged, trying to look indifferent, but Pen could see the troubled look still on his face. "*It was meant to be harmless. Missing supplies. Messages on the wall. I had nothing to do with the ladder,*" he insisted. "*That was a simple accident, but after that, I refused to do any more harm. The place was...cursed. I felt ill just being there.*"

He certainly wasn't the only one.

"*But you still felt guilty,*" Penelope said. She arched a brow and gave him a skeptical look. "*I assume you didn't tell the police about that?*"

He returned a sardonic look. "*No, of course not, but they knew all the same. I don't know how.*" He scowled.

Penelope had a pretty good idea which anonymous source had informed on him.

"Did she tell you why she wanted you to do it?"

"*She wanted to stay here in Antibes—not marry that man*

*in England. She thought if her mother was preoccupied with
the hotel, she might postpone the marriage. I suspect she was
waiting for something."*

Most likely for Finlay to die of whatever was ailing her
so she could be with George.

"Where did Lily get the money from?" Pen asked.

"She is rich," Marc said, as though the question was
stupid.

"No, her mother was rich. Lily had no money."

"But George did, or at least he had easier access," Benny
said with a smirk.

*"And unlike Lily, he had every reason to tell the police
about your bit of sabotage."*

"Monsieur Martell?" Marc said, incensed.

"Oui," Benny said dryly.

*"Did you tell the police about what you witnessed
between George and Lily?"*

"It was the only reason they let me go."

Pen couldn't fault him for that. It was relevant to Vera's
murder, after all. It was also relevant to Finlay's that took
place the next day. Lily wanted her mother dead, George
wanted Finlay dead. Together, they had even more of a
reason to want both women dead. In retrospect, the police
had probably arrived at the Martell residence to arrest
George for the murder, not Finlay.

*"Did you tell the police about your argument with
Finlay?"* Penelope asked.

Outrage flashed in his eyes. *"Why would you ask such a
thing?"*

"Because I saw it happen. Why was she upset with you?"

His mouth twisted with resentment before he
answered. *"She thought I was being too intimate with Lily. I
don't know why she cared, even though it was not true. Yes,*

obviously, she is a beautiful girl. But as you and I know, her interest was elsewhere. She was quite upset about it, even when I denied it. She told me to stay away from her. I finally had to tell her that I was not the one she should be worried about. She asked me what that meant, and so I told her."

"You *what?*"

He shrugged. "*She left me alone after that, but she was not happy.*"

"So Finlay knew, or had reason to suspect George was being unfaithful with Lily." Penelope looked at Benny, who had already come to the same conclusion. This explained perfectly why Finlay would want to frame George for her death.

"*As I said, femme fatale,*" Benny hummed.

"*Did Lily tell you anything about her relationship with Finlay?*"

"*We did not talk much, especially not about her. I understand. Americans are so stiff about such things. Here, a man takes a mistress and it is not an issue.*"

Unless he kills his wife to be with that mistress, Pen thought to herself.

"*I should go back now,*" Marc said, giving them an expectant look.

"*Yes, of course. Sorry to intrude on your day.*"

He rolled his eyes and rushed back in before Penelope could change her mind.

"So now at least we know why Finlay would want to frame George," Benny said. "Hell hath no fury, and such."

"Yes, but it doesn't explain why she'd kill herself."

"And perhaps more importantly, why now?"

"The timing *is* interesting. At least the second time around, taking the laudanum, we can determine both a motive and method. She wanted to frame George, now that she knew about his affair with Lily. We also determined how she could have gotten the poison in."

"But the night of the party, she wouldn't have had a motive to frame George. Also, how did she get the poison there? I assume she didn't hold it in her mouth the entire night," Benny said in a droll voice.

"No, and she had no purse or other means of carrying it. Which means it must have been someone else." Pen nibbled on her thumb to consider the other possible suspects. She instantly grimaced at the taste that met her tongue. She remembered touching the dirty backroom door in the store and gagged in disgust.

"Are you alright, dove?" Benny asked with a small laugh.

"Hardly, I need to wash my—" Pen stopped when a sudden memory hit her. "The gloves!"

"The gloves?"

"The night of Vera's party, it looked as though Finlay had spilled some of her drink onto her gloves. There was also a splash on the front of her dress. I assumed both were from some of the drink having sloshed over the side of the glass. What if the dose of poison was in her glove? It was either soaked in the fabric or inserted into her drink through a hole in one finger. Either way, whatever that poison was, it must have left a mark or had some effect on her skin. I'd wondered why she was wearing white gloves the day we went to visit. After all, we were mostly in the shade of that sunroom. She was covering up the evidence of her poisoning."

"*Mon dieu,*" Benny crooned. "Surely, by now the doctor examining her body would have noted that."

"Yes, which means the police would have eliminated the source of at least one of the poisons. I'm guessing it was arsenic in Finlay's case. We know that leaves sores on the skin. It would have also given her enough time before death to dispose of or at least wash the gloves free of evidence."

"Which still leaves the cyanide, and who put it in the drink."

Benny and Penelope stared at one another, both of them coming to the most obvious conclusion: Lily Tynehook.

CHAPTER TWENTY-NINE

It hadn't taken much persuasion on the part of Benny to have Penelope join him on a sleuthing mission to the Hôtel de Platine. She only felt guilty about the fact that they were about to publicly uncover Lily's motive for killing her mother.

"Do you suppose she knew George was slowly poisoning Finlay?" Benny asked Pen in the taxi ride to the hotel.

"I doubt it. He would have no reason to tell her."

"True, and now he may very well make out like gangbusters. There ought to be a law."

"I agree. At the very least, she should have thought to write him out of her will before she poisoned herself."

"Odd that she didn't," Benny said, turning to her with a frown.

"What if...she did," Pen said, her mouth slowly dropping as it dawned on her.

"Tell-tale, dove, tell-tale!" Benny said, eager to learn what Penelope had just discovered.

"All along the timing for everything has bothered me.

Why did Vera buy the hotel when she did? Why did she come to Antibes in the first place? Why did Finlay change her will so recently? Why did the poisonings happen when they did?"

"*Well*?" Benny asked impatiently.

"You of all people should know the answer to this, when does the social season end in London?"

"Does anyone really bother with that anymore?" He wrinkled his nose at the outdated notions that had certainly lost favor since the Great War, when seemingly everything in society changed.

"You do if you're older, and have always had a fascination with British society."

"Ahh, well in that case it follows Parliament, or when the Royal Family is in residence. Usually, it ends sometime in July, no later than August."

"And for a young lady set to get married at the end of the season, at least according to her mother, there would likely be a period of shopping in Paris for her trousseau. Yet another outdated notion someone like Vera would cling to."

"Which didn't give Lily much time. So, she poisoned her mother to prevent the marriage. We've always known that much."

"But what we haven't known thus far is Finlay's motive for poisoning herself. That would have to take us back... almost eighteen years ago."

Pen waited for Benny to latch onto what she was suggesting. It didn't take long, his mind easily sliding to the most scandalous of notions.

"You think Lily was Finlay's daughter!?"

"It's the most obvious conclusion. The new will specifically mentioned children born to her naturally. That would include any who were eventually given up for adoption. Finlay was sent to a supposed 'health retreat.'"

"Ah yes, one of the more notorious euphemisms for many a familial embarrassment."

"Exactly. George thought it was a euphemism for a sanitarium. But no, I suspect it was because she'd found herself in a delicate condition—after a summer spent with a red-headed beau. Lily even stated that her mother had her dye her hair a blonder color to be more appealing to men. Perhaps from the slightly redder color it truly is?"

"Oh my stars, this is quite the cornucopia of dirt," Benny said, pursing his lips. "So then, Sawyer is Lily's uncle?"

"By birth, at any rate."

"But didn't Lily tell you she was adopted at five? That her parents had died in a car accident?"

"What if they were simply the *original* adoptive parents? I think even Lily might not have known they'd adopted her from a seventeen-year-old Finlay, forced by her family to give her up."

"But how would Finlay know? Aren't those things usually done anonymously?"

"Unless you're someone with both money and power. Vera has a penchant for learning everything she can about anyone worth knowing."

"Yes," Benny said sourly.

"Why wouldn't she know everything about the five-year-old girl she was adopting to be a companion for her daughter?"

"And the private investigator Finlay's lawyer hired. She wasn't looking into adopting, she was looking into past adoptions!"

"Very good, Benny," Pen said in a teasing voice.

"Patronize me all you want, dove, but some of us are naturally inclined to find dirt. You should include me more often."

"I should."

He waived it off, eager to continue uncovering more clues. "So, Vera learns that Finlay is Lily's real mother. Is that why she bought the hotel?" He frowned in confusion. "But why now? Surely, she's known this all along?"

"She has. But according to the gardener, Alec, Finlay has been meeting with this private investigator since before the Tynehooks even arrived in Antibes. I think some sort of alert was set in place, informing Vera that Finlay was looking into finding the daughter she had been forced to give up so many years ago. Perhaps it was her inability to have children that made her feel so compelled. He must have found proof, if Finlay changed her will so recently. That's what set all of this in motion."

"Do you think Lily knew?" Benny asked.

"I doubt Vera would have told her, or George for that matter. That's if he even knew." Something about that flicked an irritating loose end in Penelope's head. She dismissed it, continuing to follow the thread she currently had a hold of. "At any rate, Vera came out to ensure there would be no scandal—or, worse, Lily's financial independence—to ruin the marriage that would finally realize her dreams of British aristocracy."

"How would she have done that? Buying the hotel just seems...a bit zealous. And not particularly effective. All it did was make Finlay angry."

"True," Penelope considered that. Why did Vera buy the hotel? What else had she done to ensure Finlay wouldn't meddle?

Any answer to those questions was forgotten as the taxi

slowed down now that they'd reached the hotel. Both Penelope and Benny were surprised to see several police cars out front.

"Is that Lily in handcuffs?" Benny asked.

The question was pointless as it was quite obvious that the police were arresting her. She was marched to one of the police cars by two policemen, while Inspector Cloutier and M. Gérard Travere looked on.

However, what drew the most attention was Prynne becoming hysterical at the front entrance. "No! It wasn't her! She didn't do it! She couldn't have possibly done it!"

Julia and Peter were doing their best to hold her back as she tried chasing after her sister. Lily was surprisingly stoic as she was shoved into the back of one of the police cars. As Penelope caught a brief look at her face, she noted her expression was just as neutral. It looked as though she was numb to the charges levied against her.

Penelope and Benny quickly exited the car and rushed over to where Peter had finally taken hold of Prynne, who was still struggling to run after her sister.

"What happened? Why have they arrested Lily?" Penelope asked, already suspecting the answer.

"They think she killed Mother!"

"It's nonsense, of course," Julia said.

"Of course it is," Peter said in a reassuring voice, trying to settle Prynne who had finally sagged against him. The concern and adoration were practically etched onto his face. Lulu was right, Penelope was positively blind when it came to noting secret affection.

"I have to follow them, tell them they have it all wrong," Prynne whimpered. "*I* should be the one taken away. Lily's suffered enough."

"Don't be foolish, Prynne. For heaven's sake, pull yourself together!" Julia brought her hands up to turn Prynne's face her way. "This *will* be resolved, you have my promise on that. We both know she didn't do it. I'll make sure myself that the police let her go."

That seemed to have a calming effect on Prynne, and she nodded.

"Did they at least give a reason why they thought Lily may have killed her?" Benny asked, doing a fine job of looking more concerned than nosy.

"Prynne, I think we should go inside. You need to rest," Julia said, more to Peter than to Prynne.

"Some nonsense about an affair with George Martell," Prynne blurted out, ignoring her. "It's absurd, of course. Lily had no interest in him."

Both Penelope and Benny maintained their poker faces. It was pointless to bring up everything they had discussed on the way there. It seemed the police had come to the same conclusion they had: Lily was the second poisoner.

CHAPTER THIRTY

"It doesn't seem right," Cousin Cordelia lamented.

Penelope and Benny had returned to the villa to update everyone else on what they had learned, including the news of Lily's arrest. They were all in the living room, sipping drinks and musing over the latest developments.

Penelope had to agree with her cousin, it was a sad affair. George was a vile mercenary sort, but Lily was still so young. At that age, girls were easily wooed, especially by handsome, charming older men. George had probably even used his wife's illness as a means of currying sympathy and admiration for braving through it all. It wouldn't have taken much pressure to push Lily to the point of murder, especially for a woman like Vera Tynehook.

"The worst part is, it seems George may actually get away with what he's done. Finlay was the one to poison herself, or attempt to, both times. Never mind that he'd been trying to poison her for his own nefarious means for months before that."

"Do you suppose he knew Lily was Finlay's daughter?"

Lulu asked, posing the same question Penelope had wondered.

"How? He didn't even know she'd given birth when she was younger."

"Perhaps he did," Richard posed. "Remember when he interrupted her as she worried aloud that she thought she was being punished? I assume that was for giving up her daughter for adoption."

"Yes, it does seem odd that a wife wouldn't have told her husband about it, the man she at one point loved and trusted," Lulu said.

"Hmm, I suppose it could have been a cover, him claiming this health retreat was really a sanitarium because she'd, as he suggested, tried something like this before," Penelope said.

"But again, we have no proof. And even if he did know Finlay had given birth, he wouldn't have known that girl was Lily," Richard said. "As Benny said before, those hushed adoptions are usually anonymous."

"But Vera knew, of course she did."

"But she is no longer alive to say as much," Cousin Cordelia pointed out.

"She must have told someone. The men she hired to learn about Lily's origins? Julia, who seems awfully close to the family? Maybe even Prynne?" Lulu said.

"Or...George," Penelope said. The loose thread that had bothered her on the way to the hotel was now something she could grasp. "Vera came to the Martell home one time. George was the one to meet with her, according to Sara, the housemaid. What if he wasn't telling her they wanted nothing to do with her or her plans for the hotel? What if they were coming to an understanding?"

"An understanding?" Cousin Cordelia asked. "But

surely he despised her as his wife did? After all, she'd bought their hotel."

"I don't think he cared much about that hotel. That was Finlay's project. His sole aim was money, and Vera would be the one to sniff out an opportunist. She knew Finlay was searching for the baby she'd given up, and there could only be one reason for that. She probably laid it out for him quite plainly, Finlay's inheritance was in danger of being split, or worse, left entirely to Lily. If Lily were to find out, she'd have no reason to marry the earl she despised. And the earl might not be so keen to marry a girl whose background was so...tawdry. It's one thing to be adopted from a married couple who tragically died. It's entirely different to be born to a seventeen-year-old out of wedlock. So Vera would have encouraged George to put a stop to it."

"By any means necessary," Benny said in an ominous tone.

"But he didn't," Lulu pointed out. "Finlay was the one to poison herself."

Penelope considered that. "I think he was accelerating it. He wanted her to put the wallpaper up in her bedroom again. And those books that surrounded her, they were probably covered in arsenic."

"Even the silk flowers, the leaves might have had the green dye laced with it," Richard said.

"What was he waiting for? It gave Finlay enough time to discover that Lily was hers, apparently," Benny said.

"More importantly, why not eliminate Lily? She was the most pressing obstacle to his fortune," Lulu said.

"Vera would have instantly known it was him," Pen said, shaking her head. "He'd be the only one with motive, no matter how much he made it look like an accident. No, I think this secret tryst of theirs was the key. Accelerate

Finlay's mysterious illness, then deal with Lily. Perhaps even another marriage followed by—"

"Another murder, just as cleverly disguised," Benny finished.

"Except Finlay had other plans."

"I hate to sound like a tedious refrain, but..."

"We have no proof," Penelope finished for Richard. She sighed in frustration. Nothing about this case—both of them—felt like justice. Even if Lily had been the one to poison her mother, one couldn't help but feel sorry for her. She'd been used by both her mother and George. Now, her short, miserable life would end in prison, or worse. France still used the guillotine. Penelope shuddered to think of it.

"The good news is, this lack of evidence works both ways," Richard said. "All they really have is Lily's affair with George and her desire to avoid the marriage her mother had arranged for her. As far as we know, they have no solid evidence that she was the one to put that cyanide in the glass."

"I hate to rely on the goodwill of a jury," Penelope said. "Though, I suppose that's how these things usually end."

They all pondered that, no doubt picturing Lily's fate. Their thoughts were interrupted by the announcement of a knock on the door. Irma answered it and was handed an envelope sent by courier. Everyone in the living room watched her read the front of the large envelope, then carry it into the living room.

"It is a letter for Mademoiselle Banks and Detective Prescott."

Penelope was closest so she took hold of it and opened it. Inside there was an envelope, the standard kind that correspondence was delivered in.

"It's from the Office of Edwin Clark," Penelope said in surprise after pulling it out and reading the front.

"Well, open it," Benny said, making sure Penelope didn't do something terrible like read it in private.

Penelope couldn't imagine what secret information the attorney would have to impart, knowledge that shouldn't reach the ears of notorious gossips. After all, she and Richard only spent less than half an hour in his office, and had been summarily dismissed, with prejudice.

"I'm curious as well," Richard hinted.

"Oh, I suppose," Pen said. She quickly tore the envelope open and pulled out several sheets of paper. The first had a rather short, concise statement that she read aloud:

To Miss Penelope Banks & Detective Richard Prescott,

Enclosed you will find a letter, copied from the original, written by Mrs. Finlay Martell (née Schroeder). On June 12, 1926, at 11:47 a.m. I, Edwin Clark, received a phone call from Mrs. Martell. During that call, she instructed that, under specific circumstances, I was to make several copies of the previously written, enclosed letter and send them to various individuals, including yourselves. I was also told to inform you of said circumstances under which the letter should be sent, one of the two scenarios:

1. The arrest of Miss Lily Tynehook for the murder of Vera Tynehook
2. The arrest of Miss Prynne Tynehook for the murder of Vera Tynehook

As I have been made aware that there has been an official

arrest of Lily Tynehook for the murder of Vera Tynehook, I am obligated to remit the enclosed letter.

Please note, other than this statement explaining the circumstances under which the enclosed letter from Mrs. Finlay Martell was to be remitted, I provide no comment, addendum, or any other statement that should be construed as legal advice, personal commentary or opinion, or involvement in anything beyond the copying and sending of Mrs. Finlay Martell's handwritten letter in her own words. I have simply dispensed with the final wishes of my client.

I will provide no further comment on the matter, which you may now consider closed.

Regards,
Advocat Edwin Clark, Attorney at Law.

"The date and time of the phone call, that was when we were visiting her home!" Penelope said.

"She must have made the call when she left to change," Richard said.

"And take the laudanum."

"But what does the enclosed letter say!" Cousin Cordelia demanded.

Penelope quickly set aside Mr. Clark's letter to find another, longer typed one, presumably the words of Finlay Martell:

I, Finlay Laura Martell (née Schroeder), do hereby confess to

*poisoning Vera Tynehook on the evening of June 11, 1926. I
stored a lethal amount of arsenic in my right glove and laced
my drink with it. I then handed it to Prynne Tynehook, who
had no knowledge whatsoever of the poison, knowing that
she was delivering it to her mother.*

*You will find those green, satin gloves in the second drawer of
the dresser in my bedroom at my residence. There will be
enough evidence of the arsenic remaining to qualify as
evidence.*

*My original intention was to commit suicide that night. I
had recently been made aware that my husband George
Martell had slowly been poisoning me with arsenic for
months. I suspect this was in an attempt to gain control of
the entirety of my inheritance. Perhaps an autopsy will show
evidence of this before I am finally laid to rest. The doctor
my husband recommended me to, going by the name Dr.
Hugo Archambault, there is no record of him having a
license to practice anywhere in France. This "doctor" has to
date been unable to diagnose what was wrong with me.
Now I know why. He was conspiring with my husband to
kill me.*

*A visit to a real doctor, Dr. Cedric Breguet, confirmed that I
only had months to live. The exposure to arsenic has taken its
toll.*

Penelope stopped reading to stare at the others, all of whom
also recognized the name.

"That's Vera's doctor, isn't it?" Lulu said.

"It is. And he was obviously able to diagnose what was wrong with Finlay."

"But not Vera?" Cousin Cordelia asked in confusion.

"I suspect he did, but she chose to keep it a secret for some reason."

"Leverage," Lulu said. "She knew something in that hotel was causing it. Hell, that doctor probably pointed her right to it. That's how she got George Martell to work with her."

"Yes, it makes so much sense!" Penelope said, angry at Vera all over again. "She deliberately kept the information from everyone, including her own daughter who was exposed to it!"

"Vile woman!" Cousin Cordelia said, then gave an abashed expression. "May she rest in peace."

"It's quite the coincidence, Finlay picking the very same doctor, don't you think?" Lulu said, one eyebrow raised.

"I don't think it was a coincidence at all. Just one more final move in her game of chess. I suspect there are two Tynehook sisters that have received this same letter. She would have wanted them to know the full extent of their mother's nature."

"Ahem," Benny interjected. "Does said letter have any more to impart?"

"Oh yes," Pen said, quickly returning to the letter. She continued reading:

I know there was another dose of a second poison in the drink that killed Vera Tynehook. I saw my husband George Martell put it in himself. At the time, I assumed it was some sedative, as I had become hysterical earlier in the evening. Now, I know he intended to complete what he had gradually been doing for the past several months: murder me via poison. Vera Tynehook was the victim of that poison, originally intended to kill me.

I am confessing this freely and voluntarily, and with sound mind, to my attorney Edwin Clark as my witness. I have given him instructions to present this letter to the police when the circumstances require it, even after my death.

Signed,
Finlay Laura Martell.

———

"Well there you have it," Richard said. "That's certainly enough to persuade any jury that Lily isn't guilty, whether it's true or not."

"You think she's lying?" Cousin Cordelia asked.

"I think she has no reason not to, particularly that bit about her husband being the one adding the second dose of poison."

"How would she even have known about the second dose? You and Penelope only told us because we weren't possible suspects."

Penelope was the one to answer her cousin. "She knew because she knew it wasn't her arsenic that had killed Vera. If she really had intended to kill herself that night, she would have naturally researched the manner of death, including how long it would take and the symptoms. What we all witnessed was very different from anything she would have expected."

"It could only have been someone else adding a dose of another, quicker form of poison," Richard said.

"And why not blame her husband?" Lulu said, not bothering to hide her smirk of admiration.

"Really, who could blame her?"

"Remind me never to upset you, my dear," Richard said.

"You're the one who pointed out it's usually the spouse who is the likely culprit."

"And now it seems Finlay may have given George the same death sentence he laid on her. The statistic remains unchallenged."

"Yet another reason to never marry!" Benny said lifting his glass up.

"Is it true, do you think?" Cousin Cordelia asked with a frown. "Did George really put cyanide in Finlay's drink?"

Penelope and Richard eyed one another.

"I think ultimately, it was a mother protecting her daughter and the only other person in the world who truly cared for her, Prynne. Whatever guilt Finlay felt about giving Lily up for adoption, especially considering the childhood she had, she atoned with this final act. The church may not approve, but I, for one, applaud her. It's fitting, if not exactly justice."

"Hear, hear!" Lulu said, lifting her glass.

One by one, the others joined in, echoing the same sentiment.

EPILOGUE

This time, Penelope came alone. She found a way around to the back of the Hôtel de Platine and was pleased to see Prynne alone in the garden. She paused, then quietly approached, not wanting to startle her.

"You don't have to sneak up on me," Prynne said, her head still bent over a bush, inspecting the leaves.

Pen came to a stop, wondering how she'd been noticed.

"The lavender," Prynne said, raising her head and turning to face Penelope. "I'm familiar with the scent. It's my favorite."

"Of course," Pen said with a small smile.

"I suppose I know why you're here," she looked off toward the sea. "And I suppose there's no reason now not to tell you what you want to know."

Again, Penelope found herself surprised. She had expected to work much harder for this.

Prynne turned to fully face Penelope, tilting her head to study her. "It must be nice having so much wealth at such a young age. But even before that, you were quite independent, traveling the world, defying your father, getting a job, even gambling to make ends meet."

Pen blinked in surprise, which caused Prynne to smile knowingly. "My mother was nothing if not thorough. She did her research on you, learning everything she could in anticipation of hiring you to investigate what was happening at this hotel."

"And everything she knew, you knew as well. Including the fact that Lily was Finlay's daughter."

Prynne's only response was a humorless smile. "Don't be mistaken, I wasn't a confidant. I was...simply there. Even more than Julia, once I was an adult."

"Which meant you were there the day your mother had a private meeting with George—which I suppose is where he learned about Finlay's little secret?"

"And where I learned a few things myself." Prynne's expression became steely, something Pen had never witnessed in her before. "Like the fact that George had been secretly poisoning his wife for months."

"How...?"

"How did I know? Because Mother knew it was the wallpaper. Why do you think I took you and Detective Prescott by it that day? She knew the signs of poison. You see, my mother had been doing the same to me since I was born."

Penelope gasped.

"Not arsenic, of course, and just enough to make me sick, not kill me. At least I don't think so. I wasn't supposed to have figured it out. I suppose Mother thought all those years of sickness also affected my intelligence. The moment she told George she knew what it looked like when a person was poisoning someone, it was like a lightbulb went off for me. She knew because she'd done it herself. Any time a medical professional threatened to glean what she was doing, another specialist would come in to replace him."

"Oh, Prynne."

She waived Penelope's sympathy away. "When father died, she had something else to occupy her time. Another way to air her grievances in life. Of course, she had always tried to intervene in his business affairs. She thought she knew better. Perhaps she was right, as she has been quite successful. Far more than he was. Who knows what would have happened had he not had that sudden heart attack?"

Prynne paused to focus on a leaf with which she was fiddling. That left the air pregnant with meaning. Penelope didn't dare ask if she thought—or knew?—Vera had killed her husband.

"Lucky for me, I gained a sister," Prynne said, brightening up and turning back to face Penelope. "I also suddenly began feeling better. I was never back to perfect health, and probably never will be. Everyone attributed the change to Lily. Now, I know it was just that Mother didn't have the patience to make my health concerns her personal albatross."

"So, you learned all of this during that meeting your mother had with George when you two went to the Martell home?"

"Yes."

"Did you tell Finlay? The police?"

"Finlay, of course. I...I thought it was *her* place to tell the police. I said I would confirm whatever she told them. I don't understand why she didn't go to them."

"She obviously had her own form of justice planned."

"Perhaps she was right," Prynne said, shooting Penelope a defiant look. "George was trying to kill her. What does it matter if she finished what he started? And why? All so he could have complete access to her money? She was devastated when I told her the truth."

"And then she did you and Lily the favor of taking the fall, even after death."

Prynne's brow creased in confusion. "We didn't do this."

"I can understand not wanting to incriminate yourself or Lily. Even with Finlay's confession, I suppose there's always a chance—"

"No, I mean it," Prynne insisted.

"So, you really believe George was the one to add the cyanide?" Pen was incredulous.

Prynne studied her for a moment, then turned back to the bush she'd been looking at when Penelope arrived. "Mother was horrible to everyone who had the misfortune of coming into contact with her."

"Peter?"

Prynne paused before answering. "Peter came here because of me. We met when Mother was looking to buy any theater Lily might dare to run away to. He was the one to suggest a ruse that Mother would appreciate. We knew marriage was hopeless at the time, but at least, if we were careful, we could be near one another. Mother liked having control, especially over something successful like one of his musicals."

"I suppose he doesn't have to worry about that now."

Prynne's mouth hitched up on one side. "As I said, he wasn't the only one who took issue with my mother."

"Julia?" Pen's eyes widened in realization. "She was going to turn herself in that day Lily was arrested, wasn't she?"

Prynne stared out past the garden to the sea. "Julia has been with our family long enough to know what Mother was doing to us, at least most of it. She didn't know about the poisoning. She truly thought I was sick all that time. Selling Lily off to that...man. All because he had a title? Learning what she'd done to me was the final straw, I suppose."

"Did you see her poison the drink?"

"No, and I'm certainly not stating she *was* the one to poison the drink, either." Prynne pierced Penelope with a firm gaze. "Frankly, it could have been any of us. Or perhaps it *was* George. At least one witness has claimed as much."

"Prynne...."

"Finlay confessed. That's all that matters. The people who should be punished will be, soon enough. The rest of us would like to get on with our lives, or finally have lives of our own."

Penelope struggled with that, but the point was moot. The entire investigation had suffered from a lack of evidence and a firm candidate on which to lay the blame. Finlay had solved that problem. She'd even managed to inject an ironic sense of justice into the matter.

But Penelope had one more question.

"Did you know Lily was Finlay's daughter?"

Prynne stared at her, eyes unwavering. "I've always known. I thought it wasn't my place to tell either of them. In both instances, it felt like a betrayal to the other person. That's the one thing I regret now. Perhaps...I don't know...."

"One thing I've learned is that there is no point in wondering 'what if.'"

Prynne gave her a weak smile. "That doesn't stop it from happening."

"No, I suppose it doesn't."

"Lily's forgiven me. I'd like to think Finlay has as well."

"Your actions are hardly unforgivable. What are your plans now?"

"We're selling this hotel. That's the first thing. Lily and I are going to Paris. It will be our first taste of independence."

Penelope smiled. "It's a fine city to experience it."

"It's going to be more complicated returning home. Lily is with Sawyer and Estelle, or Amelia Hobson I should say. She's informed me she will be taking on a stage name when she finally makes it to Hollywood." Prynne cocked a half smile. "She's teaching Lily everything she knows about the world of acting. They're quite close now, despite everything. As for Sawyer, Lily is learning what little she can about Finlay, particularly the way she was once upon a time. Her father as well, though I doubt he wants to have anything to do with her."

"You of all people know family can be complicated."

"I suppose I do," Prynne said with a sigh.

"But you have Lily."

"We have each other." She gave one final sigh and turned away with a smile. "Good day to you, Miss Banks."

AUTHOR'S NOTE

Anyone who has read enough Ernest Hemingway or F. Scott Fitzgerald will recognize the setting of this novel. For a brief period between the World Wars, many Americans did in fact take over that part of France, particularly Antibes, making it their home. It was only natural that Penelope and crew would do the same at some point.

I've drawn from various sources in my research for this book (and, of course, took certain liberties).

THE MARTELLS

This couple is very loosely based on Gerald and Sara Murphy, who bought a property on the rocky cliffs of Antibes that they named Villa America. However, when they first arrived in 1923 they rented the Grand Hôtel du Cap (see below) for an entire summer to entertain their friends. That began the interest in the south of France as a summer destination rather than only a winter one.

In F. Scott Fitzgerald's book *Tender is the Night*, he bases his characters Dick and Nicole Driver on the couple, who were friends of his.

THE HÔTEL DE PLATINE (The Platinum Hotel)

The hotel in this novel is based on the real life hotel that is now named Hôtel du Cap-Eden-Roc in Antibes. It was originally opened as a private mansion in 1870 under the name Villa Soleil. It sat abandoned for 17 years until an Italian hotelier brought it back to life as a hotel in 1889. It was then modernized in 1903. Many famous people have been guests at the luxurious hotel, including the Murphys (see above), King Edward VIII and Wallis Simpson (who originally wanted to get married there), Marlene Dietrich, and the Kennedys.

ARSENIC IN GREEN PIGMENT

Beginning in the late 18th century, particular shades of green pigment were made with products that produced a copper arsenite. It began to fall out of favor after the 1860s when people realized the toxic effect it had. The pigment was quite popular, used as a colorant in everything from clothing to paint to wallpaper and even silk flowers.

An illustration from 1862 entitled, "The Arsenic Waltz," shows two skeletons in period dress for a ball. The female has a crown of fake flowers and a large gown with fake flowers attached. It was meant to represent the effect of arsenical dyes in clothing at the time.

I first learned about this deadly pigment during a tour of The New York Society Library. One of the book binding rooms in back had temporary possession of a set of green books affected by this toxic dye. I was fascinated with the idea of someone dying from a love of reading! Though, the tour guide assured us that the levels of arsenic in the covers was minimal, I still knew I had to incorporate it in one of my books.

GET YOUR FREE BOOK!

Mischief at The Peacock Club

**A bold theft at the infamous Peacock Club.
Can Penelope solve it to save her own neck?**

1924 New York
Penelope "Pen" Banks has spent the past two years making
ends meet by playing cards. It's another Saturday night at
The Peacock Club, one of her favorite haunts, and she has

her sights set on a big fish, who just happens to be the special guest of the infamous Jack Sweeney.

After inducing Rupert Cartland, into a game of cards, Pen thinks it just might be her lucky night. Unfortunately, before the night ends, Rupert has been robbed—his diamond cuff links, ruby pinky ring, gold watch, and wallet...all gone!

With The Peacock Club's reputation on the line, Mr. Sweeney, aided by the heavy hand of his chief underling Tommy Callahan, is holding everyone captive until the culprit is found.

For the promise of a nice payoff, not to mention escaping the club in one piece, Penelope Banks is willing to put her unique mind to work to find out just who stole the goods.

This is a prequel novella to the *Penelope Banks Murder Mysteries* series, taking place at The Peacock Club before Penelope Banks became a private investigator.

Access your book at the link below:
https://dl.bookfunnel.com/4sv9fir4h3

ALSO BY COLETTE CLARK

ABOUT THE AUTHOR

Colette Clark lives in New York and has always enjoyed learning more about the history of her amazing city. She decided to combine that curiosity and love of learning with her addiction to reading and watching mysteries. Her first series, **Penelope Banks Murder Mysteries** is the result of those passions. When she's not writing she can be found doing Sudoku puzzles, drawing, eating tacos, visiting museums dedicated to unusual/weird/wacky things, and, of course, reading mysteries by other great authors.

Join my Newsletter to receive news about New Releases and Sales!
https://dashboard.mailerlite.com/forms/148684/72678356487767318/share

Made in the USA
Coppell, TX
06 April 2024

30996664R10144